Moving Parts

MOVING PARTS

STORIES

LANA PESCH

Arsenal Pulp Press   Vancouver

MOVING PARTS
Copyright © 2015 by Lana Pesch

US edition published 2016

ARSENAL PULP PRESS
Suite 202–211 East Georgia St.
Vancouver, BC V6A 1Z6
Canada
arsenalpulp.com

The publisher gratefully acknowledges the support of the Canada Council for the Arts and the British Columbia Arts Council for its publishing program, and the Government of Canada (through the Canada Book Fund) and the Government of British Columbia (through the Book Publishing Tax Credit Program) for its publishing activities.

Canadä

This is a work of fiction. Any resemblance of characters to persons either living or deceased is purely coincidental.

Moving Parts was previously published in *Little Bird Stories Volume I*, September 2011. *Who Does That?* (an excerpt from "The Rogues and Scoundrels among Us") was published in *Little Bird Stories Volume II*, May 2012.

The quotation on page 5 is from *The Left Hand of Darkness* by Ursula K. Le Guin, copyright © 1969 by Ursula K. Le Guin. Used by permission of Ace, an imprint of Penguin Publishing Group, a division of Penguin Random House LLC.

Cover photograph: "la ronde" by Jane Heller
Design by Gerilee McBride
Edited by Susan Safyan

Printed and bound in Canada

Library and Archives Canada Cataloguing in Publication:
Pesch, Lana, author
Moving parts : stories / Lana Pesch.

Issued in print and electronic formats.
ISBN 978-1-55152-624-9 (paperback).—ISBN 978-1-55152-625-6 (epub)

I. Title.

PS8631.E794M69 2015   C813'.6   C2015-903346-2
                                               C2015-903347-0

The only thing that makes life possible is permanent, intolerable uncertainty; not knowing what comes next.
—Ursula K. Le Guin

CONTENTS

MOVING PARTS

She waited for him. It was two in the afternoon, and she sat at one of the wooden, new-made-to-look-old tables. She ordered a soda water that came in a tall glass with a black straw and a slice of blood orange. Fancy, Edie thought. Fancy water, in a trend-setting restaurant, for the clever folk of the West Queen West Toronto neighbourhood. All the waitresses were actors, their hair twisted up in haystacks with chopsticks poking out. Messy cool, like Montreal.

A Lululemon family sat by the window. The svelte mum with painted-on eyebrows and neutral-coloured lips thumb-typing on her BlackBerry while Daddy fed the kid whole wheat Cheerios from a baggie. The toddler's stroller, boy or girl, Edie couldn't tell which, blocked the aisle. No one was bothered by this.

Edie dipped her pinky finger and the one next to it into her water and tried to flick out her hair just above her ears. Messy minus cool. Was this church pew bench made of concrete? She lifted both cheeks off the seat by pushing her hands down and extending her elbows, then lowered herself back down. She shifted side to side to the bossa nova remixes piped into the room, but nothing made the hard seat more comfortable. She waited, praying he would show up here, at the United Church of Gentrification.

They had met at No Frills, the supermarket on Lansdowne. In her peripheral vision, while in the lineup at the cash, she caught him eyeing the contents of her red basket. Bananas, green beans, jumbo olives, raspberry kefir, and a box of Jell-O pudding (vanilla). She became self-conscious about the Jell-O. Edie had been feeling a cold coming on, and this was a thing from her childhood; her mother had made it for her and her sister when they got sick. Edie later learned that milky sweet treats were not at all helpful in getting rid of a cold. Lemon tea with ginger and Cold-FX capsules was what her mother should have given them. Edie knows better now. She knows she should be buying those things, not vanilla pudding. But her mother had let them eat in bed and watch TV past their bedtime, and they never stayed sick for long. She nudged the pudding box behind the bag of beans.

As she got closer to the cash, Edie turned and pretended that she was looking past him. He looked like he might be in a band. Maybe he was one of those guys who sat at a drafting table, drawing plans for buildings using different kinds of rulers and special pencils. He smiled at her then and she was forced to smile back. It was one of those polite smiles she gave to gas attendants or cashiers or salespeople who accosted her at The Body Shop. It all seemed pretty grocery-store normal. Not flirty at all. Not until he tapped on her window in the parking lot while she was letting her car warm up.

With a gloved hand, she rolled down the window.

"I never do this," he said.

He was hunched over, craning his neck, careful not to come too close. His teeth were remarkably white. Straight as a toothpaste ad. Edie was not afraid, or offended, or particularly flattered which, she thought later, maybe she should have been.

"Okay," she said, drawing out the second syllable of the word.

"Do you, uh…do you want to…maybe meet for coffee sometime?"

She met plenty of perfect strangers on a regular basis—volunteers she organized at work, people at Scrabble tournaments, out walking the dog. But none of those strangers had ever asked her out.

"Oh," she said, "Um." She adjusted the fingertips on her green wool glove and tucked her lower lip under her top teeth. This was weird.

"I know this is weird," he said.

It looked like he was going to say something else but instead turned and watched a car drive out behind him. One hand was shoved in the pocket of his cargo pants and the other carried a recycled grocery bag that she knew contained—from having also checked out his basket back in the line—bananas, a carton of skim milk, Quaker oatmeal, a glass jar of whole-grain mustard, and a box of Triscuits (original). His hair was curly and light brown, like a wheaten terrier's, and he had on a tan corduroy jacket, almost the same colour as his hair, with a furry collar that was used and pilly. His jacket was undone too far for such a cold November day.

He was nodding as he spoke, "But I said to myself, Ditch, you've got a fifty-fifty chance here."

If he were an animal, Edie thought, he would be a chipmunk. Cute, a bit jittery, harmless.

Edie hadn't been on a date since Joey, the disastrous blind date that Sandra had arranged. Sandra met Joey while temping at HSBC during tax season. He had recently broken up with someone he'd been with for eight years, which was all he talked about when he and Edie met at a Russian martini bar. During drinks, a line of spittle stayed connected between his lips when he went on about Julie, the ex. Overactive salivary glands. Edie knew the name for this, ptyalism, from doing crossword puzzles. At one point, when Joey was near tears while talking about their old neighbourhood, a blip of drool ran down his chin and fell right into his Sputnik Appletini.

Going in blind was one thing. At least here, with the chipmunk, she could see what she was in for. What's the worst that could happen? They go out and have a great time? They like the same foods and discuss documentaries because they are both members of the Revue Cinema? In three years, after some debate, they try to have a baby. They have a baby. They name him George, partly because of the curious monkey and partly because they are both Orwell fans. George grows up to be a male Jane Goodall, and Edie and Ditch spend their retirement years in Kengoya—an African fusion country (Congo plus Kenya), because by 2030 the Chinese have taken over a lot of the continent, but Canadians and Australians have automatic POW (Peace of Way) status from the Chinafrica Immunity

Act (the CIA)—running George's gorilla sanctuary. They tend to the apes who are named after Canadian towns like Digby, Terrace, Sherbrooke, and Wawa. They eat stewed gumbo and bitter chocolate. They drink strong coffee with goat's milk, and in the evenings, they play Scrabble in the gazebo protected by mosquito nets. Edie wears her hair in a long grey braid and Ditch, now bald, never takes off his safari hat. All their clothing is cream coloured and made from natural linen.

Or, they could meet for coffee and realize they have nothing in common other than the fact they both bought bananas at No Frills.

Then she said, "Yeah, okay."

His eyebrows lifted. "Okay?"

"Sure," she heard herself say, followed by, "Why not?"

He waited for her. It was fifteen minutes past two o'clock. He filled his glass with water from the vodka bottle the waiter had brought over. A sprig of rosemary floated inside it like a plastic fish. It was a crap shoot, Ditch knew that, but he had to try something. It had been nearly two goddamn years since he'd been on a date. Then his colleague Peter, the host of the morning radio program Ditch worked for, practically advertised it on air one day.

"What, really? A good-looking guy like you, single?" Peter had said.

Thank you, Peter, for that.

"I wouldn't think you would have any trouble meeting someone."

"Well, you know, busy-busy, always on the go," Ditch said while they were still live.

Of course he wanted to meet someone. Who didn't? Come to think of it, when was the last time Peter had been on a date? Ditch had hoped, secretly, that things might have picked up because of the embarrassing on-air comment. But the most he got was a few sarcastic Tweets and several questionable Facebook friend requests.

Later that week, he saw her in the lineup. Pixie haircut, vintage leather coat, bananas, green beans. Maybe it was simpler than he thought. He had grown up in a tiny prairie town where, because there were so few of them, people talked to each other. Standing there behind her, it occurred to him that he was losing those small-town sensibilities. He used to strike up conversations with complete strangers all the time. On a crowded subway car where people were jammed up against each other, he'd try to lighten the mood and say things like, This is a sporting event, right? Full body contact! Or, on Monday mornings, while getting a coffee to go, he'd tell the cashier, Cheer up, it's almost Friday.

Just say something to her.

But in the express line, Ditch could only muster a smile. Now that he was secure in his professional life as a reputable sports journalist, making decisions in his personal life was becoming increasingly difficult. He was even having trouble with small things. When Dove stopped making the moisturizer he liked, he had stood for twenty minutes scanning the options in the lotion aisle. Couldn't he just slather on some Noxzema and be done with it? He ended up taking the advice of the drugstore employee with heavy eyeliner at the makeup counter and paid over a hundred bucks for a small jar of Biotherm. She said the face cream was enriched with something-*ylase* that was going to help battle the toxins found in urban environments. "It's for puffiness and dark circles," she talk-whispered. "You know, right here," she said, patting under her own eyes as if she were giving a forbidden tap to the side of an aquarium.

Ditch checked the time on his iPhone. Two thirty-five. Was she standing him up? Perfect. That would be just perfect. Was she just another egocentric Toronto woman who led him on then left him hanging, for no good reason? He had been excited, hesitant to admit he was giddy, after their phone call. He had hoped Edie might be different, with her vintage style and anti-technology ways. Who doesn't have a cell phone?

Or was there a good reason?

Maybe she'd been hit by a bus on her way here and was lying on a gurney in a hallway at St. Mike's because there were no beds left. Maybe her leg was broken and she was lying there thinking selflessly, Who is going to walk my dog? Ditch imagined her being excited to go out with someone new, do something unexpected, with a guy who asked her out in a parking lot. He had approached her in the parking lot. Who does that? It's creepy and stalker-like, now that he thought about it. Now that he thought about it, he *really* should have talked to her in the lineup. That's what a normal person would have done. Of course she was having second thoughts. She probably wondered what else he was capable of when he wasn't busy approaching unsuspecting women. She probably thought it through and realized he could be into roofies or secret basement rooms or collections of strange beetles he'd captured and tacked to bits of cardboard and framed behind glass.

Yeah. He was getting stood up.

Five minutes before three o'clock, Ditch asked for his bill. He paid for his Funghi Assoluti and tipped the waiter fifteen percent. She took the cash from the faux leather folder and wished him a nice afternoon. "Well, I doubt that," Ditch said under his breath. Nice, not nice, what did it matter? He would never be back here. He was never dating again.

Outside, his corduroy coat hung open in the cool afternoon. He'd done laundry and had worn his short-sleeved brown T-shirt with the Atari symbol over a long-sleeved white T-shirt. He looked casual good, like he was ready for a first date. But seriously, why bother? Why even make the effort? From now on, he was going to cook his own goddamn chicken soup and watch National Geographic documentaries by himself. Who gives a crap about finding someone special to—

Wait a minute.

Weren't there two Terroni locations?

Edie stood on the sidewalk outside the restaurant. She should have known better. When they spoke on the phone last week she detected something in his voice she couldn't quite put her finger on.

"I lived in Montreal for five years," he had said.

"And you can't speak French?"

"How did you know?"

"It happens," she said.

Through the receiver she thought she heard water running. Was it a toilet flush? She wasn't going to ask.

"Well, yeah. So. You're lucky."

"It takes practice," she said, and added, perhaps too quickly, "It's a commitment."

She chalked it up to nerves. Something she hoped he might be experiencing too. But she had been looking forward to this.

Yet here she stood. Stood up.

Behind her, The Sunny Pawn Shop window was crammed with abandoned items. A guitar, an old blue chair, a pyramid of digital camera boxes, and a jewellery display with a ruby ring the size of a lozenge in the middle of it. She rested her hand lightly on the glass, inches from the guitar. She might learn to play one day. Maybe today, now that she had had a change of plans. Maybe if she got good enough, she could play at those variety nights they had in bars with exposed brick walls on streets like this. Maybe she could find somewhere to fit in. Maybe, when she performed, she could wear colourful knitted hats and sparkly scarves and a white tank top (like Feist used to). Maybe she would find something worthwhile to—

"Edie!"

The sides of his corduroy jacket flopped out behind him like a cocker spaniel's ears. He narrowly dodged pedestrians on the sidewalk like ski markers on a downhill slope.

"I was at the wrong one!"

He was still two blocks away but he was loud.

"Hey, Edie!"

He charged full-throttle toward her, and she couldn't suppress her smile. The muscles in the front of her neck tensed up, in a good way, as her plans changed once again.

Parts of it happened then.
Parts of it happened later.
Parts of it happened like this.

Edie sits beside him in the stands of the soccer stadium. They have very good seats, not that she would know the difference between a good seat or a poor seat as she has never before attended a professional sporting event. It's a step up from watching roller derby, she knows that much. The clouds, staggered in shades of grey and blue, hang over their heads. Ditch is working. He scribbles on his notepad, recording strategies and style, players' numbers and positions that will be included in his report the next day. Never in her life, Edie thinks, has she been so close to people who make as much money as these athletes. When the game pauses, she leans over and rests her head on his shoulder. He stops writing for a moment, turns his head, kisses her hair.

After, they go back to Ditch's place where he makes the meal he knows how to make best. Baked trout with green pepper slices on brown basmati rice.

"The secret is whole-grain mustard," he whispers, displaying the jar.

Edie nods and sips her glass of pinot grigio. She still remembers the small glass jar of mustard he had in his grocery basket when they met over a year ago. She marvels at the two of them now, together like this, and can't picture the random encounter ending any other way. Perched on the stool facing the kitchen where Ditch cooks, she swings her leg, tapping a socked toe against the counter, and allows the wonder of it all to rest silently in her heart.

DEFFER'S LAST DANCE

Uncle Deffer is the kind of guy who tells you about the kind of shit he had. I mean that in the most graphic and literal way: he takes pride in every detail.

"Little rabbit turds floating there," he'll say. "Pinched off like Hershey's kisses."

Or once: "It was a perfect goddamn heart shape. Where's a camera when you need one, eh, Max?"

He'll say this out loud at the dinner table or standing in line at the grocery store. Then his laugh will turn into a cough, and he'll lean over to support himself with whatever is around—the counter, his denim-clad thighs, or lately, me.

There's a tennis match on the TV in here. Federer and Nadal are trying to outsmart each other. Tricksters. Women's tennis is so much better, and I don't just mean for the skirts. As a healthy male in my early twenties, I can appreciate a good sporting event, but these guys hardly ever get a volley going. I mute the game with the remote, silencing their boar-like grunts. Last time I played was with my ex-girlfriend, Mandy. Ended up knocking the ball over the fence every time, and all she could say about my game was that I was all power and no technique.

"Ease up, Max!" she'd say, annoyed.

It was instinct to smash the ball as hard as I could when it was coming at me like that. Smash the hell out of anything coming at me like that. I told myself, Okay, listen to her, she's better than you. Next shot, take it easy, you don't need to kill the thing. Then, wham! Popped it straight up in the air like a cheap firecracker.

"What the hell?" she said, laughing. Same thing she'd say when I was fucking her.

I'm sitting in the common waiting area on the first floor of the hospital. Beside the TV is a dying fern and a bookshelf lined with old paperbacks. There's a small room adjacent to the emergency exit with a sign on the door that says FAMILY ROOM in black letters on a gold plaque. Mom's in there now, lying on the couch with a cool cloth on her forehead. Over by the fridge there's a small sink with a Dixie cup dispenser, and I'm trying to ignore how much I want a cigarette by focusing on the hum of that fridge. I've seen nurses open it: it's full of juice boxes and individual containers of applesauce. Across the way, someone is having a coughing fit that sounds like it won't end well.

Federer with his cheesy headband and Nadal showing off his biceps—the sweaty bastards never even crack a smile. It's a twenty-first century duel with a foofy audience applauding in their crunchy whites and TAG Heuers. Elites hiding behind their aviator sunglasses making bets on which gladiator is going to fall.

It went like this. Friday night—last night—I was having an early dinner with Uncle Deffer at a greasy spoon on Yonge

Street. He was hitting on the waitresses and ordered his usual plate of liver and onions and a Labatt 50, and before he could ask for a slice of coconut cream pie he starts having the worst headache of his life.

"I'm dying here, Max," he said, leaning over his plate.

He was holding his head in both hands. I mean, it was that sudden and that bad. Then he started puking right there on the carpet, and one of the waitresses called an ambulance. Next thing I know, it's the next morning and I'm sitting in a pea-green La-Z-Boy down the hall from his hospital room.

Federer smashes the ball over the net at like, what, 140 miles an hour? Cocky son of a bitch knows how good he is. You can see it in those beady brown eyes. It's a confidence that can't be taught. Mandy had it. Deffer, too. But serving is only half the battle. What's the defense plan, man?

Last night I followed the ambulance straight to the hospital in my car without going to my apartment and called Mom at her place after Deffer was admitted. She paid fifty bucks for a cab even though I told her not to rush.

It's been a long night, and I can't tell if it's the vending machine coffee or the Walmart lighting in here that's giving me the shakes. Outside, in the park across the street, a couple of kids are hanging upside down on a jungle gym. I wish I hadn't texted Mandy. I'm going to close my eyes just for a minute, take a short break from it all—a break from Mom's anxiety, from replaying the Specialist's speech about how the first forty-eight hours of care are the most critical. Deffer hasn't moved a muscle all night.

I can't help thinking how this is like buying a magazine with an article you really want to read, say, *Wired*, with a piece on the value of applied research. You're reading along, and when you turn the page to finish the article, it's gone. Like, the page is physically not there. It's been torn out, and when you go back to the store where you bought the magazine, pissed, all the snotty clerk can say is, "Sorry, sold out." Now you're even more frustrated so you go home and try to find the thing online and all you get is: HTTP 404—File not found.

I rub my eyes with both hands, and when I open them, there's an old guy sitting across from me. He's wearing a green and yellow John Deere baseball cap with mesh on the back and a navy windbreaker with an iron-on patch that reads: Frank's Car Sales. He's picking little pieces off his Styrofoam coffee cup and eating them.

"What the hell?" I say, looking around to see if anyone else thinks this is odd, but there is no one around. Dude's a bit grey. The colour of wet rock.

"Thought I'd come down for a cuppa joe and a snack," he says.

He crushes what's left of his cup and stuffs it in his mouth. Pats his bloated belly and limps over to the vending machine because one leg is slightly longer than the other. He flicks the tops off, like, ten sugar packets, tears them open, and shakes the contents into his mouth.

"Do you know my Uncle Deffer?"

"I know a lot of people, kid."

He's pudgy and round and looks like a sickly version of the

animated Santa from *The Year Without a Santa Claus*, but without the beard. Unsteady on his feet, he's like a kid learning to walk. He licks his blueish-purple lips and wobbles back to his chair. When he passes me, the thumb of his left hand falls off and lands on the floor. It rolls under the La-Z-Boy.

"Jesus," I say.

"Darn it," he says.

The Corpse bends down to get the thumb, and a wicked odour hits me. He smells like a litter box that hasn't been cleaned in weeks. I push my nose into the elbow of my sleeve. He finds the thumb and squishes it back onto his hand like a piece of Plasticine. He lets go and flexes it a couple times. "Good as new!"

"It's not even straight."

"Left hand," he says, waving his hand around like he's at a concert. "Close enough."

He shakes his hand out more aggressively, and I'm afraid his thumb is going to come off again.

An EMT gets a coffee from the vending machine. Padded soles of nurses' shoes in the hall next to us. The choppy clank of a portable IV drip rolls by. I realize no one else sees the waving Corpse but me.

"So what's your deal?" I ask him.

"I'm under oath."

"To who?"

"It's complicated."

He does a full-body shimmy like a dog shaking off water, and white flakes that look like coconut fall out from under his ball cap.

"I'll bet," I say.

"Kind of a non-disclosure, non-compete kind of thing."

On the TV, the game has ended. Nadal scrunches up his face like he's been sucking on a lemon while he shakes Federer's hand. C'mon, Nadal, be a man. Winning a fat cheque isn't going to get you any further ahead. You did your best. You played hard and you lost and so the fuck what?

"Bravo, Max," says the Corpse, "Very nice."

"What?"

"Sounds like you're getting the hang of this."

"Of what?"

"Exactly."

The Corpse nods his head, grins, and goes over to inspect the selection of paperbacks.

"I'm going for a smoke," I say.

"You sure you want to do that?" he asks without looking up.

It's a bright, cool October day, and the kids in the playground across the street are stalking an insect or something in the leaves. They're doing a crouch-and-move routine trying to catch it. First, the boy reaches for it with both hands, but the thing gets away. Then the little girl laughs, and they chase it a few feet further trying to sneak up on it. Not sneaky enough. They do the crouching bit again, but it jumps forward, just out of their reach.

Ten years ago, when Uncle Deffer got divorced from Auntie Bettie, he came to live with my mom and me for a while. I was fourteen. Mom used to send me to do the grocery shopping with Deffer, and once I saw him take a jar of roasted red peppers off the shelf, undo the lid, take a sip, put the lid back on, and return the jar to the shelf. He said it kept his blood pressure regulated.

Deffer never came right out and said why his twenty-six-year marriage to Bettie ended—nobody did—but I suspected there were other women, younger women. What I didn't understand then was why any woman, at any age, was attracted to him, especially a woman like Bettie. She looked like royalty compared to our family. A pale-skinned, dark-haired China doll that might break if you hugged her too hard. She was manicured and sophisticated and she never wore jeans. Always a dress or a pant suit. But I don't think the divorce was entirely Deffer's fault. Our gender is partly to blame. Some of us are pigs. Some are dogs. The worst: pig dogs. Deffer? Man-child at best. Maybe it was his lack of filter that Bettie loved about him. That, and the guy could dance.

When I closed the deal on my condo last year, I had a party on the rooftop patio. Mandy, Mom, Deffer, my friend Ben from work, and his girlfriend. Back then, things were good with Mandy, and I was starting to see a future for us. She moved in, sort of, but didn't pay any rent. She rolled up all my towels and lined them up in one of those straw baskets from IKEA. Plugged vanilla air fresheners into all the electrical outlets and filled the front closet with shoes. For the party, I downloaded some old-style dance tunes especially for Deffer—waltz, two-step, foxtrot—and brought my speakers up to the patio. Deffer waltzed with Mandy first, and while Mom was talking about some new massage client, I kept an eye on them. Deffer's charm could be contagious; I saw how Mandy was flirting with him as he deftly maneuvered the two of them around the patio furniture. The heel of his hand was pressed into the small of her back so she had no choice but to follow his lead, which she obviously enjoyed. Her head was tilted at a sly angle, exposing the long side of her neck, and when he spun her around, out came her slut face! Lips puckered and slightly parted, squinty eyes. What the fuck? When the song ended, Mandy's hand lingered on Deffer's shoulder a beat too long. She walked back to where the rest of us were standing, all flush and giddy like she'd just got to lick the pudding bowl clean. When Deffer shouted, "Who's next?" Ben's girlfriend shot over to him like a bullet.

Later, Deffer and I were standing by the safety rail having a beer and looking out at the city lights.

"You did good, kid," he said, "Helluva place for someone your age."

He popped me in the shoulder and held out his Labatt 50 for a toast.

"Proud of you," he said.

I clinked my bottle to his. Then he nodded in Mandy's direction.

"Your girl there likes to lead, huh?"

Back in the waiting area, the Corpse is watering the fern from a Dixie cup. He steadies himself with one puffy hand on the TV, dead leaves falling everywhere.

"Know when to fold 'em," says the Corpse.

"You're making a real mess in here."

"The trick is knowing when to clean it up."

"How is that a trick?"

He goes to the sink and fills up two more little cups.

"These plants don't get enough water," he says, spilling the water because of his uneven gait. He's right. It's super dry and the heat is cranked too high. I go over and start sweeping the leaves and dandruff under the bookshelf with my boot.

"That's not getting rid of the mess."

I kick at the stuff more aggressively.

"You're just hiding it."

"Oh, for Christ's sake."

Things started to sour with Mandy about six months ago when she insisted we take up an activity together. She said that ordering pizza and watching *Arrested Development* over and over again didn't count; it needed to be something outside the apartment.

So I went to the tango lessons.

Given Deffer's ability on the dance floor, I guess Mandy expected that I would have some skill. His rhythm was flawless, his timing absolute, and he had even tried to give me a few pointers once at a family wedding when I was eleven years old, but it soon became apparent that those genes had skipped a generation. I was the wallflower at school dances and when I got older, I faked my way through club nights by sticking close to the bar. Or, if I was forced to dance, I pulled out a kind of seizuresque routine and hoped no one would call me on my freakish style.

Our tango class was led by a square-shouldered Argentinian with the face of a bull. His partner was a tiny blonde thing in a body-hugging black leotard. At our first Tuesday night class, he lifted her straight up above his head, holding her by her teeny waist. Her red skirt fell in his face when he let her down, then he flung her around the side of his own washing machine of a body. No way in hell was I going to attempt that with Mandy. Not with her control issues.

During their next instructor demo, the two of them moved around the room like water. Like nothing else existed. Their legs circled and swirled into figure eights, tracing invisible infinity symbols on the floor, like the tattoo on Mandy's wrist. Oozing tension and lust like that, they must've had sex in the back room during the break. I felt my dick shift a little when they swept past Mandy and me standing with the rest of the students. With Mandy's tendency to lead combined with my lack of coordination, we looked like a B-list comedy act, as far from sensual as you could get. At the second class—our last class—when Señor Torro came around to assist us with the basic slow-slow-quick-quick-slow move, Mandy said to him, "You should see how good his uncle is. I don't know what's wrong with him."

In June, she took her shoes and her vanilla and moved back in with her folks in Oakville, and I'm back to folding my towels like a normal person.

My eyes well up and I start to pace, a habit inherited from my mother. I go to the sink and pour myself a Dixie cup of tap water. *The first forty-eight hours of care are the most critical.* Another day, and the only father figure I've known might be gone. When I was four years old, my dad died in a freak accident when a tire came off a transport truck and flew over the meridian on the westbound QEW, landing smack in the middle of the windshield of his Chevy Impala. He died instantly. My mother never got over it.

I look in the cupboard under the sink and find a plastic dustpan and brush. I go back and kneel down, start sweeping the leaves and the dandruff or whatever into the pan. The Corpse picks up a ratty copy of *The Alchemist*.

"I wish there was an almanac in here," he says. "The charts help my eyes stay focused."

I sweep up small pebbles that roll around in the dustpan like the granules from my mom's homeopathic medicine. They've got Deffer on a cocktail of drugs I can't even pronounce.

"The first forty-eight hours are critical," the Corpse says.

"So I hear."

The Corpse grumbles, coughs, and horks up a ball of phlegm. He pinches his lips together and shuffles to the garbage can and spits. Bits of Styrofoam are embedded in the mucus. My stomach tightens, and I try not to gag.

"Excuse me," he says.

"I should've helped him more."

I wipe my eyes with back of my hand because I'm still holding the brush.

"Try not to blame yourself."

"Have you seen him?"

I'm sweating now. I take off my jacket and toss it on the back of one of the metal chairs.

"Yeah," the Corpse says.

"What's the plan? Pump him full of drugs and hope for a miracle?"

He takes a wrinkled handkerchief embroidered with orange and yellow flowers out of his pocket. It's frayed, and the threads are all coming out; when he wipes his lips, a piece of orange string hangs down from the corner of his mouth. Holding the dustpan full of garbage in front of me I face him square on.

"How much do you know about all this?" I ask, pointing at him with the brush.

"You mean why is the floor so filthy?"

My armpits are moist. I stare him down like a cat. No blinking.

"I mean the treatment."

I open my mouth and lick the side with my tongue in an exaggerated way to show him that he's got something on his mouth. He pulls at the thread, holds it up to examine it, then drops it into his mouth like a strand of spaghetti.

"Is it going to do anything?"

He bobs his head from shoulder to shoulder, somewhere between shaking and nodding while he's chewing on the string.

"Or is it just prolonging the inevitable?"

"It's the oath kid, I—"

"Fuck your oath."

"Maybe you should keep your voice down."

"Maybe you should give me a straight answer."

"Now, now." He swallows the string. "You don't need me for that."

Fucking dead trickster is as bad as Federer on the tennis

court. The Corpse's left knee buckles, and he puts his arms straight out at his sides to balance himself. He's a regular circus act. A hairball the size of a plum slips out from the bottom of his pant leg. He picks it up and places it in my dustpan.

"Pardon me," he says.

When we got to the hospital last night, Mom and I met with the Specialist in the FAMILY ROOM. After she told us how critical the first forty-eight hours were, she suggested we stand at the end of Deffer's bed and pretend like he was there with us. Not him now, incapacitated and unconscious, but as he was a month ago, living with me in my condo before any of this happened. She said to imagine him standing there with us, looking down at his unconscious self.

"Ask him what he thinks you should do," the Specialist said.

What would Deffer say about a still-life version of himself on a whack of blood thinners with a feeding tube in his arm and oxygen being pumped into his body through his nose? He'd ask for a beer, a whisky, and a shave. He'd ask what his chances were, and when the Specialist said, "Not good, I'm afraid," he'd say, "Pull the plug and put this bed to some goddamn use."

But I didn't tell her any of that because I am in love with the Specialist. I hope to hell Mandy won't show up because of that stupid text. If she does, I'll tell her it was an accident and she needs to leave. The Specialist is like no one I've ever met. She is an extraterrestrial land mermaid with an iridescent brilliance surrounding her that makes it impossible to look away. She is a fairy tale so perfectly sculpted it puts her at risk of being kidnapped, or proposed to, or stabbed to death. And when the Specialist had asked us to imagine what Deffer would say if he were standing there, it was my mother who answered.

"It's not like we haven't dealt with death before. Tell her, Max."

The Specialist was glowing. She was lit up with a kind of radiance that offset the despair of the hospital. She was a super-hero, and I couldn't stop staring. It was like I'd been hypnotized.

"I had a cockatiel once," Mom said.

The Specialist looked directly at my mother when she spoke and said, "Try to think about what he would want."

"I'm just saying," Mom said. "That bird had a stroke and lived for another two years. Comfortably."

Mom punctuated the last word by snapping her fingers very close to the Specialist's face.

There was no defense plan. The Specialist wasn't trying to outsmart anyone. She was giving Deffer some temporary relief with that cocktail of drugs she'd prescribed. The Specialist was no trickster, she was just trying to prepare us for match point.

I called in sick today and my manager gave me her standard reply of, "Okey-dokey, Champ." I do the regulatory filing for the Canadian divisions of companies like P&G and Pfizer. Everyone needs to be accountable, and everyone else wants things accounted for. I'm under oath—like the Corpse, in a way. A confidentiality clause in my contract forbids me from invest-ing in certain companies because I am privy to embargoed news releases that report their earnings. No problem in my book. I push the papers, but I don't have to agree with their work. Contrary to what Mandy chose to believe, I have morals. And I figure there are worse things I could be doing with my math degree.

I've had five cups of coffee now, and all the powdered creamer has made the inside of my mouth feel like the cotton batten in a dollar-store gift box. I dump the contents of the dustpan into the garbage, ignoring the revolting ball of phlegm, and go to the fridge for juice boxes. Apple for me, orange for the Corpse.

If Deffer does by some miracle pull out of this, there's a woman at the office who I think would be a good match for him. She wears slippers to work under her long flowery skirts. Her name is Sara. She's pretty in a retro kind of way. Sometimes, in the hall, she bumps into the photocopier or a cubicle partition because she's always looking down at her feet. In the lunchroom, she eats tuna right out of the tin, holds it up to her face and pokes around at the meat with a fork. She mumbles things like "deadlines" and "routine," and when people say "Good morning" or "How are you?" Sara doesn't say anything at all. Truthfully, I'm jealous. I respect her slippers and her tuna and her zoned-out attitude. I wish I could be more like her. I wish I could be more like Deffer.

"Amen to that, brother," the Corpse says.

He is sitting in the La-Z-Boy now, flipping through the channels with the remote. I hand him the box of orange juice and turn away.

"Thank you kindly," he says. He takes the straw off the box and uses it to clean out his ear.

"Can't you at least use some Febreze or something?"

"Oh, sorry about the smell."

He pushes the recliner back and crosses his ankles. He's not wearing socks; under his loafers the skin on his legs is a yellowish green and scaly, like an iguana's. I almost reach out and touch it.

"Just to be clear, you're never going to give me a straight answer."

I finish my juice box and keep sucking after it's empty, making a loud noise. The Corpse seems pleased.

"Not my call," he shrugs.

There is a tightness in my chest that won't go away, and his non-responsive answers are cranking me up even more.

"I'm more … facilitator than informant," he says.

I head for the door. I need a smoke.

"Thanks for the clarification."

"Things are going to get real clear, real soon, buddy."

As the hinged door closes behind me, he belches and adds, "But you don't need me to tell you that."

The Christmas I was seven years old, Deffer got so drunk he sang all the way through dinner. He scarfed down his stuffing and sang between mouthfuls, keeping time with the heels of his cowboy boots under the table. He clacked his cutlery against Mom's good china and howled out various renditions of "Good King Wenceslas." Then he made me and my cousins stand on our chairs and sing-whisper "Silent Night" in rounds, directing us like a real choir director. He said standing on our chairs made us more like angels, got us closer to heaven. It was a Christmas miracle, and my mother cried and dabbed her eyes with a napkin covered in red and green stockings.

Earlier this morning, we stood by the door to Deffer's room, and the Specialist handed Mom a Post-it. The Specialist was not intimidated by my mom, who can take up a lot of space for someone five-foot-four including the frizz on top of her head. Mom changes jobs and boyfriends like most people change socks and underwear. Even though her therapist encourages her to *live in the now* and *project the image you want to attract*, Mom has never been able to commit to anything or anyone since my dad's tragic and unexpected death. She has trouble focusing and gets distracted because of all her ideas. Some of her inventions have been: drinking glasses with built-in coasters, noiseless flip-flops, and a solar-powered hair comb/pocket knife/flashlight/compass. She is bonkers for The Shopping Channel.

"Don't look at it," the Specialist said after handing over the little yellow piece of paper. "Pretend you found this in his pocket and he had written his wishes on it."

"Oh, for Christ's sake," Mom said.

She crumpled up the paper and threw it at the garbage can in the far corner of the room. It bounced off the wall and landed on the floor.

It's two p.m. Forty-eight hours minus sixteen. Mom has gone outside for a walk. She's doing laps around the hospital, pacing in circles because she doesn't want to go too far. I'm out of smokes so I bum one off the guy in the wheelchair outside. We don't talk. The kids in the park are chasing each other around a climbing apparatus. The little girl almost catches the boy, but he hurries up the ladder to the slide. He waits for her momentarily, then shimmies down before she can tag him.

I should probably eat something, but the apple juice and the nicotine have given me a second wind. I'm still thinking about the Specialist when I come back in to the waiting area, which is now overpowered by an artificial orange smell. She is every Hollywood crush I've ever had. Replace her lab coat with a flowing white gown, and it's that scene in *Lord of the Rings* where Galadriel and Frodo are in the forest and he offers her the ring because he wants no part of it. I want no part of this. She's my Galadriel, special effects and all. A magical filter surrounds her, setting her apart from the rest of us mere mortals.

"You're getting distracted, Max," the Corpse says, standing by the TV.

"You're going to tell me what I should be thinking now?"

I sink back into the La-Z-Boy.

"Now is the time to focus."

He positions his hands like a film director framing up a shot. There is a cracking sound, and his right arm breaks off at the elbow. It falls forward inside the sleeve of his jacket. I go to grab it, but he snags it with his left hand, mismatched thumb and all.

"Nice catch."

"Not the first time," he sighs. "Won't be the last."

"What do you mean, focus?" I ask, strangely feeling the need to impress him.

"Be a man."

He turns and walks unsteadily toward the FAMILY ROOM, and I notice an aerosol can of Citrus Magic sticking out of his back pocket. The TV is still muted but TSN is recapping highlights of the earlier tennis match. A short clip shows Nadal standing there with his head hung low after he failed to return a serve, a look of defeat on his face.

How does the Specialist do it? How does she put up with the abuse from people like us? She must have to deal with this kind of thing, like, 500 times a day. I bet she's married to some Zen yoga master. A completely mindful motherfucker who is devoted to his perfect wife and, after so many years, still finds meaningful ways to renew the connection that brought them together in the first place. He probably hides unexpected gifts under her pillow so she finds them before bed. Maybe a new smock made from fair-trade cotton because in her spare time— when she is not dealing with sad sacks like us or mentoring new staff or doing research for her book: *Palliative Care: The Real End Game*—the Specialist paints watercolours. I want to drown the Buddhist bastard in a pool of lotus flowers.

"Easy there, popcorn," says the Corpse.

His windbreaker sleeve is wrapped up with silver duct tape and looks like a bad upholstery job.

"You're falling apart."

"Who, me?"

He smiles and one of his brown front teeth drops to the floor. It bounces like a thumbtack. He bends down to pick it up. "I'm fine."

"Be a man, you say."

"I do say."

He pushes the tooth back up into his gums. I trace the stubble of my beard with both hands. Slap my face a few times. Squeeze my cheeks together and massage my jaw. The Corpse is right. Things are becoming clear.

"This is so fucked up." The words are muffled from me pushing my face together into fish lips.

"Bingo," the Corpse says and taps the end of his nose. He bites down once, twice, makes sure the tooth stays in place. "Now we're getting somewhere."

Around three-thirty, I fall asleep in the La-Z-Boy and wake to the touch of the Specialist's hand on my shoulder. The ephemeral touch of a fairy. She says my mom has gone to use the washroom and pulls a chair up next to the recliner. The Corpse is nowhere to be seen. I pop a green square of mint gum into my mouth. The kids across the street are on the swings now, propelling themselves higher with every pump.

With a voice like whipped cream, the Specialist tells me that there is a thirty-day mortality of ten to fifty percent after an intracerebral hemorrhage like the one my Uncle Deffer has suffered. Then, slower, she explains how more than a third of patients who experience this type of stroke don't survive.

"Honesty is more helpful than giving you false hope," she says.

"Right, okay. Sure," I say, chewing. I want to bolt. I want to join the kids in the park.

"As I said before, it's this initial time of care that is incredibly important."

She speaks with the precision of a box cutter. I can see she believes that I am more level-headed than my mother. I am the adult here. *Be a man.*

"Of course."

I chew my gum, snapping it against my front teeth with my tongue, and think how Deffer would be flirting with her if he were awake. He'd be bragging about his crap. He would make the nurses hang on to his bedpan until the Specialist made her rounds so he could show her the remnants and they could examine the feces together, discover the mysteries within.

"He's more of a friend than an uncle," I say.

I use the word *friend* when what I really want to say is *dad.* She places one of her exquisite hands on my forearm and I want to shrink into a miniature version of myself and climb inside her lab coat and never come out. I want to live in there, in her magical castle, and eat tomato soup and grilled cheese sandwiches and wear flannel pyjamas and slippers, like Sara from work.

Instead, I feel my dick getting hard.

"I understand," the Specialist says.

"Do you?" Mom says.

I almost wish it were the Corpse. Mom is back from the washroom. She starts to pace back and forth in the waiting area.

"It's my job to understand," the Specialist says.

She is the fucking Dalai Lama.

"Then I guess you understand what it's like not to be able

to do one single thing about any of this?" Mom says, marching back and forth.

The Specialist lowers her clipboard. I lean my head into the flattened leather headrest of the recliner. I cover my crotch with my jacket and push out the footrest of the chair so I can cross my legs. I kick off my Blundstones, exposing one brown sock and one grey sock. I rub my face vigorously. Run my fingers though my hair. I need a shower. I need to spit out my gum. I need out of here.

"It's natural to be feeling this way."

Her voice is the single flame on a floating tea light.

"And it's frustrating," she continues. "I know that."

I can't stop staring.

"But you've got to understand something else."

It suddenly occurs to me that Deffer could remain this way for days. He could flat-line like this for weeks, maybe months, and I would be here all the time. I would get to see the Specialist every day!

"No matter what you are feeling, the final outcome is going to be the same."

I would light myself on fire for this woman. This is the opposite of how I felt with Mandy, and it takes physical effort for me to not squeal like one of those kids out on the swing set. I'm not a man, I'm an idiot. If the Corpse is the facilitator, the Specialist is the informant. She is giving me direction, honesty, truth. Game, set, match. My boner twitches.

"That's the spirit," the Corpse says. He's pulled up a chair on the other side of me. He's leaning forward with his elbows on his thighs, and I pray none of his body parts fall off and land in my lap.

"She's right, Mom." I sit up in the chair.

"What, you're going to take her side?"

"I am not taking her side." I shut my eyes hard, then open them.

"We're just another number in here," Mom says.

The Corpse is still there. I look at Mom, then at the Specialist. I'm still the only one who can see him. I speak firmly, with Deffer's confidence. It comes out as shouting.

"The outcome is all the same. I am simply agreeing with the truth!"

"Whoa there, tiger," says the Corpse. "Just lob it over the net. Easy does it."

Mom turns her back to me. Our roles are being reversed. I get up from the chair and start to pace in my socks. The tile floor is hard and cool under my feet. At least it's clean. I should give Mom a hug, but I don't. She is on the defensive, and we need to reset this game, start from zero; love. I pivot, face the Specialist.

"These thirty-day mortality percentages. What do they actually mean?"

She doesn't say anything, just slowly shakes her head, and Mom starts to howl. Even in this horribly lit waiting room of despair, the Specialist gives off a golden glow. She's wearing a peach-coloured T-shirt under her lab coat, and her blonde hair is pinned up in a bun. It's the kind of light that transforms a swamp into a magical pond, an alley into an enchanted laneway, a fool into a prince.

"So we should prepare for the worst?" I ask. No more shouting.

"Being prepared never hurts."

My hard-on wilts. I look for the Corpse, but he has disappeared again. I don't know how to do this. I don't know what to say or how to say it. Mom plunks herself in the La-Z-Boy, slumps forward, covers her face with her hands, and sobs. I feel a numbness, a stillness settling into my body where something permanent and final is taking shape.

Deffer had moved into the den of my condo a couple months ago after a rent increase forced him out of his place. He had driven a cab in the city for thirty-seven years and was living off a small pension. With Mandy gone, it made sense for him to stay with me until he found something cheaper. Mom's house was already cramped with her home-based massage therapy business and her latest venture of making monogrammed hand soaps that took up most of the bathroom and half the kitchen.

Sure, he liked his rye and ginger, and maybe we ordered too much Swiss Chalet take-out. He had quit smoking years ago, after being diagnosed with cancer of the tongue. Back then, Bettie stood by him during his treatment in her classy, silent way, preparing chicken broth and doing his laundry without complaint. When they were certain the cancer was gone, Deffer took Bettie on an Alaskan cruise.

"You better believe it, Max. Cold as a witch's tit in February up there," he told me. Then he laughed and said it could have been the ice ages and they wouldn't have noticed.

"Real passion smoulders like a charcoal briquette," he said. "You know how you tell if something is fake? Try lighting a piece of Kleenex on fire. Starts off real bright but disintegrates into nothing." He snapped his fingers to finish the thought. The cancer had given him a new perspective.

After he moved in, he took every opportunity to hassle me about my smoking. Any time I would go out to the balcony for a cigarette, he would repeatedly smack the inside of his forearm like a heroin addict needing a fix.

"There goes Max for a lung snack!" he'd say. Then he would shake his head, take a sip of whisky, and say, "That shit'll kill ya, kid."

Back in his room, we're all standing there like people waiting for the bus. Mom, zoned out, staring at the bed, finally points at Deffer's feet, still and lifeless under the sheet.

"We wear the same size boots," she says.

The three of us there together, alone. Mom looks at Deffer. The Specialist looks at Mom. I look at the Specialist. In the corner, the Corpse is cleaning his fingernails with the splintered end of a tongue depressor.

"He's never going to dance again, is he?" Mom says.

The Specialist doesn't answer.

"Maybe we should get some coffee," I say.

But I don't want coffee. I want vodka. I want to grab the Specialist's skirt in my fists. I want to pull her hips tight against mine. I want our teeth to bash together, our skulls to crack open so we can share every inappropriate thought either of us has ever had. Biting and pinching and tearing and ripping. I picture us on a drive. Summer, gravel roads, an orchard. I stop the car. She thinks it's our picnic spot, but there is no table, no bench, just a dead end. I turn off the car and go around to her door.

"Take your time," the Specialist says.

"What?"

"Take all the time you need. Get some coffee. You've been here all night. Go home for a while."

"Of course," I say.

I give Mom the keys to my car and tell her to get some rest. Take a shower. Do things normal people do when they're not waiting around for a thirty-day mortality of ten to fifty percent.

I go outside and bum another cigarette from the guy in the wheelchair. Another patient hooked up to an IV stand joins us. They're both wearing slippers the colour of plastic Easter eggs. The Corpse shuffles up behind me, pats me on the back so hard that I cough.

"Still at it?" he says.

"Today's not the day for quitting."

"You said it, pal."

Out here, he doesn't smell so bad. I butt my cigarette out in the metal contraption by the door before he says anything else. The Corpse is checking out the park across the street too. He squats down to adjust the back of one of his shoes and that's when I recognize him. He's the homeless guy who used to sit on the sidewalk outside the office. The guy who parked himself on the corner of Bay and Front at rush hour. Sat there cross-legged with a cardboard sign in his lap that read: *Will take verbal abuse for change.* He stands up, stamps his foot, and taps his nose again.

"You gave me a Booster Juice gift card once."

"I don't get it."

"I appreciated the gesture."

"What happened to you?"

"Intracerebral hemorrhage. Cerebral edema in the first twen-ty-four hours. A goner in two days."

He shrugs, spins around on one heel without losing his bal-ance, and heads for the park. A gust of wind rattles the guy's IV beside me, and I turn to see if his tubes are okay. Then a few empty sugar packets blow across the ground and land in front of my boot. I pick them up and put them in the recycling.

When I was eleven years old, Deffer tried to teach me to dance at a family wedding in Scarborough. He took me out to the alley behind Victoria Hall—it was December—and told me to stand behind him and shadow his moves. I watched him position his right hand waist-high, where a woman's torso would be.

"Two fingers here," he said. "Get this right and she'll follow you off a cliff if you lead her there."

He stepped forward and back in the slushy gravel to a song playing in his head. Out there in the cold, I tried to follow but tripped over my own feet. I stumbled and scuffed my good shoes in the muck. He never said so, but I knew he was disap-pointed. After, he let me take a drag off his cigarette.

"There is a lot you can do with just two fingers, Max."

Then he laughed so hard he had to steady himself on my shoulder.

Deffer told me that he took up dancing a long time ago because he needed to move his body after driving around in his cab for so many hours every day. Like math was easy for me, dancing was his thing. He went out to clubs and danced waltzes and polkas and two-steps. One time, I joined him at an all-ages Saturday night dance hall party where people were sashaying around the floor like it was the fifties all over again. Mandy would have freaked. Deffer moved effortlessly, poise and elegance in every turn. He led like a man is expected to. Head held high, back straight, flirtatious grin. And that's when I understood how women ended up in his arms. A single raised eyebrow was sometimes all it took. I could see why Bettie stayed.

He told me how, once, he picked Bettie up from work in his cab and drove straight to the airport. He handed her an overnight bag packed with her own things; her face turned red and she didn't say a word the entire way. They left the car in the Park'N Fly and got on a flight to Vegas he had booked that same afternoon. A package deal on a four-day getaway that included tickets to a Cirque du Soleil show because he knew it was her favourite.

We all know Deffer is not getting out of that bed.

The kids are chasing each other at the far end of the park, and the little girl stops short because something in the leaves has caught her eye. She kicks it and the boy pushes her out of the way. He picks the thing up—it looks like part of a fender—and points to the sky, eyes wide. He makes circles with it in the air above her head. Their babysitter is hunched over on a bench near the entrance of the park, texting. Her hair is the colour of bubble gum and falls forward around her face, a curtain of privacy for her and her phone.

Freshly fallen leaves crinkle under my boots. I head for the swings, passing the kiddie rides that are randomly placed in the park. There are three metal animals—a cat, a big bee, and a pig—welded to heavy coiled springs that sit on concrete slabs. The blue cat has long eyelashes and the bee is smiling; it looks moronic. The pig is painted red with a freakishly twisted-up face, and I think about the message these animals are sending to kids. The Corpse is sitting on a swing. I take the one next to him, plant my heels in the sand at our feet, push myself forward a little. Branches sway in the wind. Leaves fall and land right in front of us. High above, the chain links squeak as we move forward and back, forward and back. A squirrel scuttles past. It looks panicked, confused.

"So it just goes on like this?" I ask.

"Until it stops going."

"Never a straight answer, huh?" I laugh.

"Too easy, kid."

He flashes a brown, toothy grin at me and adjusts his ball cap. He puts his hand out toward me and I shake his swollen icy hand, thankful for his company. I'm also thankful that no more appendages have fallen off.

There's a big yellow seesaw past the metal animals, and I yell over at the kids.

"Hey, you guys want to go on the seesaw?"

They look up from the broken fender and head to the seesaw. The babysitter is still texting, still oblivious, on her bench, sheathed under a pink tent of hair.

"We're not supposed to talk to strangers," the boy says.

"Stranger danger," says the girl.

"I'm Max," I say. "I'm visiting my Uncle Deffer in the hospital over there."

"We call them teeter-totters," says the boy.

"Okay," I say.

"Seesaw is a funny name," he says.

They look at me, waiting for me to explain myself.

"It's just another word for the same thing," I say.

"Why?"

"A synonym," I say. "Two words that mean the same thing."

They stare at me.

"Like, what's another way to say something is true?"

Their faces squish up, and the boy sticks out his tongue, biting it between his teeth, thinking.

"Honest?" says the girl.

"Sure," I say. "Real, is the word I was thinking of, but yeah, honest can work."

They just stand there looking at me.

"Sad," I say. "How do you say something is sad, without saying sad?"

The girl makes a frown and crumples her brow, but it's the boy who answers. "Unhappy," he says. "Like you."

It takes both of them to even out my weight. Once they are securely positioned on the bottom end, I make sure that the girl, sitting in front, holds the handle properly. Behind her, the boy is already gripping the seat with white knuckles. There is enough room on the apparatus for his small hands to grab onto it without getting crushed underneath when they land. The hospital is across the street, but still.

"You good?" I ask them.

"Yup," she says.

"Uh-huh," says the boy.

I go to my end and pull it down halfway.

"Still good?"

Both heads nod in unison.

I straddle the plank. They're cute, these kids, like little howler monkeys perched there, waiting, ready. I bend my knees and lower myself to the ground. The higher they get, the wider their eyes open. They start to giggle, and when my end touches the ground and they reach the pinnacle in this old-school playground, they are beside themselves, hooting and hollering from fear and freedom.

Mom idles in my car at a red light, thumb and pinky alternately tapping the gearshift, waiting for change.

The Specialist advises another family on possible treatment options for their loved one.

Two trusting young souls make themselves as heavy as they can and lift me into the autumn air.

The babysitter looks up to find her kids missing.

A baseball cap sits on an empty swing moving slightly in the breeze, dead leaves swirling over the ground beneath.

And Deffer lies still. Quiet as a musical rest, his dancing boots tucked beneath the bed.

HABITS OF CREATURES

The recipe in More *magazine called for whisky. Marie had read* that a Southern tradition was to not only deep-fry whole turkeys—who owned deep-fryers that big?—but to baste your Thanksgiving turkey with alcohol. She was certain this would dry out the meat, but in order to break free from her own stale traditions, she would put it to the test. This year, there would be a store-bought pie, a big boozy bird, and a salad made from quinoa, celery, and slivered almonds with a maple syrup and tamari vinaigrette. Sophie, her eldest daughter, would be impressed. Dan would be confused.

She took a healthy sip of rye straight from the measuring cup and looked down at the list she had written on the back of a real estate notice that had come in the mail: Brussels sprouts, mashed potatoes, stuffing, new salad, cranberry sauce. She pushed her chin to her chest to stretch her neck and poked three fingers into the base of her skull with her left hand. With her other hand, she crossed off everything on the list except for cranberry sauce.

Marie took her glass of Lighthouse chardonnay out onto the back deck. Swallows popped in and out of the red plastic feeder she'd hung in the willow, their spastic grey bodies bulbous and jittery. It was early October, and things felt lighter, thinner, even with the hint of tar in the air that made its way over the tracks, a stench of toxic steam and holiday pay. The ongoing construction of the new commuter-train tracks and another condo complex was on her mental list of things she could not change, a list that also included the cat scratches on the brown leather chair, drunk drivers, the fact that her left breast was a full cup size larger than her right, a non-negotiable severance package. Just then, Gus brushed against her leg, his orange and white coat soft from the organic cat food she fed him. Gus was a stray that showed up five years ago and never left. And last year, they'd ended up with Sheldon when Hanna, her younger daughter, came home with a photo on her phone of a wide-eyed kitten up for adoption, allegedly part of a feral colony that had been uprooted because of the condo construction. Hanna named the kitten Sheldon after the character on *The Big Bang Theory* because he was actually quite brilliant, for a cat, with his fetching tricks and manic attentiveness.

Almost two decades ago, Marie and Dan were able to buy the cheapest house on the block because of its odd structure—86 Abbott looked like a barn. They loved the giant weeping willow in the back yard but always thought they would move when the girls got older, further west, maybe, closer to the park, closer to Bloor West. They'd upgrade to a place with more space, but they never did, and now they were residents of one of Toronto's hippest, up-and-coming neighbourhoods, and the price had since tripled. *Tripled.*

Slam. Clump clump clump clump clump. Bam.

Hanna.

"Dinner is in an hour," Marie called.

"I'm in the shower!"

The sky was a different kind of blue this time of year. Crisper, sharper. Like the four-pound bag of apples Marie picked up at Carluke Orchards outside Hamilton last week when she went to buy a pecan pie for Thanksgiving dinner, a change-up from her classic pumpkin pie. Dan had some special project to finish at work, so she had gone to Carluke alone. The place was an accidental discovery stumbled upon on a drive back from one of her Nature Art outings. They made the best pecan pies she had ever eaten. Pies better than sex.

Above the towering willow, swipes of cloud decorated an indigo sky and Marie let the cool climb into her. It was unusual for her to have such a lingering headache. She rubbed her right temple and sipped the wine. At her feet, Gus stared up at her; she bent down and held her fingers in front of his nose. He sniffed and his head bobbed like one of those toys in the back of a car window. Her fingers smelled of turkey and butter and Brussel sprouts, and the cat sniffed and sniffed as if she were the only person in the world.

Back in the kitchen, she sliced open the bag of cranberries with a paring knife. Tradition, she felt, was activity masked in ritual, something that continued out of necessity or need or culture and sometimes survived simply because it had been around for so long. She didn't always know where a tradition came from or why it continued. Like pumpkin pie and cranberry sauce for Thanksgiving. The berries fell like plastic beads into the stainless steel pot. She ran some water into the pot and grated a lemon over the fruit, its zest falling like fine snow. She added three tablespoons of cane sugar, turned the dial to medium, and walked out of the kitchen.

Up in the bedroom, Marie turned to straighten her top and caught a sidelong glimpse of her body in the mirror. Had she been standing next to a stack of cardboard boxes, she would be hard-pressed to tell the difference. Her skin was beige, her hair was beige, her pants, beige. Beige eyes, beige head, beige heart. Even the goddamn chardonnay had no colour.

"Blech," she said to her reflection. "Boooo."

Another running list she kept was of things she *could* change. Amount of physical activity, clothing style, calcium intake, her attitude toward the Chinese.

From the bathroom down the hall she could hear Hanna's muffled singing, although she was unable to make out the words. Marie drank the rest of her wine and set the glass on the dresser. She dug around the back of the closet and pulled out her tailored black pants. They still fit. Snugly. She replaced the V-neck T-shirt she wore with a pale blue, low-cut camisole that showed off her cleavage, and wrapped a choker of pearls around her neck. Marie fluffed out the cashmere cardigan that Dan had bought her for her forty-eighth birthday last year and brought it to her face.

Unlike traditions, usually rooted in a particular belief and associated with something pleasant, habits were either positive or negative, she told herself. Going to the gym or flossing your teeth, interrupting people or smoking crack. She had been with Dan for more years than she had been without him. Habit or tradition? Imagining herself with anyone else was like watching a scene in a movie or reading about it in a trashy romance novel. Her fantasies about Roger from *Mad Men* were all in her imagination. Fooling around was the kind of thing that happened to other people. People less beige.

She had been working freelance since last spring after the layoffs at the paper. Marie had used the opportunity to resuscitate her interest in writing poetry and to join the Toronto Field Naturalists, with whom she went on Nature Art Walks a couple times a month. The group met on Saturday mornings; they would paint or write or take photos on the outings. Back in June, she ended up going to Tim Hortons with Jared after the walk along the Don River. He was a new media grad student at Sheridan College who used the walks as inspiration for his photography. He was about a foot taller than Marie and wore plaid shirts over his T-shirts. He sported clunky black-rimmed glasses, had thick poetic lips, and spoke half the speed of anyone she knew.

"I'm thinking about getting an orchid," he'd said, sipping Earl Grey tea from his travel mug.

Jared told Marie that he had recently read *The Orchid Thief* and had become fascinated by the plant.

"They last a long time," Marie said.

"I'm not one of those guys with commitment issues," he winked.

Marie blushed. Two older women were sitting across from

them at another table. They probably thought she was a cougar. Marie turned to the women, who quickly looked away from her and went back to their own conversation. Since Dan's commitment to tennis had grown over the past year, she had decided to do something for herself. The Nature Art outings were hers; no teenagers wanting money or rides or special laundry requests. No editors making unreasonable demands. No Dan.

"It's warm in here, isn't it?" Marie said.

Jared had a calming effect. Looking at him was like looking at a good painting. A Tom Thomson—*Round Lake, Mud Bay*. That sunset over the water with the geese flying through.

"Did you know there are orchids that look like bats?"

He was a sapling. Just like the ones the city had planted along the West Toronto Rail Path to make up for those that had been destroyed after the new condo development.

"I think the sun got to me today," she said.

Jared reached over and touched her forehead and she nearly passed out. He hadn't shaved, and she suppressed the urge to reach out and touch his stubbly chin.

"You don't feel warm," he said.

She excused herself and got up. The two biddies at the other table eyeballed her all the way to the bathroom. Some cool water over her wrists should do it. A quick splash on the back of the neck. The taps were those motion-sensor kind, and even though she moved her hands in front of the little red light, no water came out. She waved them out and forward, back and forth, side to side. She took them completely away and put them back. She went to the next sink and did the same thing. She finally gave up and used a dry paper towel to dab at the beads of sweat on her upper lip.

She needed to put a cork in these feelings. What about the next outing? What if he asked her for a lift? He didn't have a car; maybe he wanted her to drive him somewhere in her Civic? She had to write down these inappropriate feelings and feed the paper to the shredder. He was hardly older than Sophie! No more coffee dates. This needed to stop. This was most certainly not going to end up in some clandestine cottage weekend where they took nature walks on hidden paths in the Muskokas. They would not end up sitting on a dock on a lake somewhere beneath a black sky peppered with falling stars. Jared would never have the opportunity to reach over and touch her forehead again or rub her stressed-out shoulders or lift those rock band T-shirts to reveal his young, flat stomach. He would not guide her hand up his long leg, his hip bone, around his lean back. She would not allow him to—

"Mom," Hanna said.

Startled, Marie slid off the bed and landed on her ankle with all her body weight. It was as if a trunk had fallen on her foot.

"Whoa, you okay?" Hanna asked.

Marie picked herself up off the floor and used the dresser for support. She flexed her foot. It wasn't broken. She smoothed out her cardigan and adjusted her pearls.

"How long have you been standing there?"

"My new conditioner smells like coconut."

Hanna scrunched her hair in a towel. Marie felt the perspiration seeping through her camisole.

"Please don't drip on the carpet." She rubbed her ankle.

"You sure you're okay?"

"What's that smell?"

"Coconut."

At least the pain in her ankle took her mind off her headache. Marie limped down the stairs in her good clothes with the empty wine glass. She hadn't put enough water in the pot and the cranberries were now glued to the bottom. She moved the pot to the sink and ran some water. Innards of a fallen lava lamp, sunken and defeated. Maybe some traditions needed to be rethought. She basted the bird once more with the whisky, took another swig, then stuck her finger in the hot pink mush and made figure eights in it. The opposite of habit, she thought— good or bad—is deviation. She sucked the sweet goo off her finger.

"Gross," Hanna said and took a box of Triscuits out of the pantry.

"It's Cajun," Marie said. "Blackened cranberry sauce."

"What?" Hanna asked, chewing on a cracker.

"Don't ruin your dinner."

"Looks like you got a pretty good handle on that already," Hanna said, taking the stairs two at a time. "Soph texted, she's on her way!" she shouted from her room.

Marie couldn't look away from her botched sauce. It was artful in a way. She briefly wondered if Jared might enjoy taking photos of the clumpy mess. Maybe a series of time-lapse photos leading up to its impending doom. Like an orchid blooming, then wilting to a slow death. Lovely-lipped, lanky Jared.

"Your father should be home soon too," Marie said, knowing that Hanna couldn't hear.

And with her favourite spatula, she scraped the burned berry slop into the organic bin.

Sophie pulled her mom's Civic over to the curb, turned off the ignition, and got out. She walked onto the stranger's lawn and put both hands on the big oak. It must be 400,000 years old, she thought. Sophie pressed her forehead against the bark and slid her arms around it. It was rough and brown, like an elephant. She'd never touched an elephant in her life. Never even seen one, except on the Discovery Channel. It must be a life-changing experience. Did they feel anything like trees? So solid and huge but walking around in that lumbering elephant way? Walking around like a big, grey wrinkly tree. Sophie burst out laughing and smacked the tree. Then, concerned, she tapped on the bark and put her cheek against its trunk.

"Who's a good boy?" she said, cooing into the rugged creases. "Who's a nice fella not going to hurt anyone?"

Sophie had spent the afternoon playing shuffleboard and eating chips in Paula's parents' basement. Her parents had left her home alone for the long weekend, and Paula had stolen the weed from her dad's secret stash. Sophie and Paula had been inseparable since grade four, and this was Sophie's first weekend home since she had moved to Kingston for university.

Sophie knelt. She ran her fingers over the tree's gnarly roots. So grounded. So connected to the earth. People needed to be more connected to the earth. This tree was sure of itself. It wasn't wondering what it should say. I love you. Do you love me? I mean *love* love me? Not like sister love. What is love? The roots were like knobs. She tried dialling them. Tried to get a signal from somewhere deep inside the planet. Channel an elephant whisperer.

A man came out of the house wearing flip-flops.

"Whoa," Sophie said.

"How's it going?"

He was forty maybe, a little on the plumpish side. A black goatee on his round face. Probably shaved his head because he was balding. He looked a lot like her Uncle Kenny.

"Awesome tree," Sophie said.

She'd taken her hand off the knobs and was stroking the bark as if it were a cat.

"Yup," he said.

"Mmmm."

She closed her eyes and imagined the elephants in India. She should just go to India. Yes! She and Paula on an adventure all their own. Riding old trains and eating curry from street vendors. It would be like their school trip to New Brunswick in grade nine, but so much better. Just the two of them. Together day and night. Like the sleepovers they had when they were kids. It was Paula who'd introduced her to cinnamon-sugar popcorn. Paula who had painted Sophie's toenails blue and showed her how to put on eyeliner. They'd used henna dye kits on each other's hair. Once, in the summer of grade seven, Sophie's dad pitched the tent for them and they had a sleepover in the backyard. Lying there in the dark under their nylon ceiling, crickets chirping all around, they made lists of which boys were absolutely kissable, which ones were maybes, which ones were never in a million years. They decided who liked who, who didn't like them back, and who was hiding who they *liked* liked.

In the tent, when Paula was asleep, Sophie leaned over and held her hand above Paula's face. She hovered over her eyelids without touching them. The tent was backlit only by streetlamps on the other side of the house, and she could barely see her own hand. She tried to transmit heat through her fingertips, communicate without words. When Paula stirred, Sophie pulled her hand away and lay flat on her back. Paula rolled toward the wall of the tent in her sleeping bag, and Sophie repositioned her body so her foot touched Paula's leg.

Uncle Kenny was still standing on the porch watching her.

"Maybe you need to be somewhere?" he said.

She definitely needed to be somewhere. India, for one. But before that, she needed to tell Paula how she felt. And before that, she needed to go home and eat Thanksgiving dinner with her family. She had another joint wrapped in tinfoil tucked in her wallet for later. In any case, the answer was yes.

"I totally need to be somewhere," she said.

Sophie stood up and got a head rush. She put both arms out to her sides for balance and saw a kaleidoscope of images crossing over each other—the tree, the elephants, Kenny, Paula.

"You okay to drive?"

"I'm good, yeah. Yeah. Thanks, though."

Sophie walked to the driver's side of the car and waved to Kenny.

"Happy Thanksgiving!"

She climbed into the car and slumped in the driver's seat. She was suddenly, overwhelmingly, famished. Not only for food, but Paula, too. What a mess. A catastrophe! A travesty. Oh, Paula. Will you love me back? Can you? Sophie sat there with the unfairness of it. Let Kenny stare. Let the elephants roam. Let her life begin!

A yellow leaf fell from above and landed on the windshield. It was curled up and tattered on the edges, an uneven dying map of veins, hinting at its former self.

Dan bent over the bed to tie his dress shoe, giving Richard one last opportunity to rub his bum, who pinched it instead.

"Stop," said Dan.

"The whisky make it juicy and succulent," Richard said.

Richard rubbed the spot he had pinched, then smacked it. He got up and covered his naked, shapely body with a brightly patterned kimono and went to the kitchen.

"What are you going to do?" Dan asked.

"Prepare mon café, make a crossword puzzle, surf porn."

If only he could buy a stupid sports car and be done with it. And he already drove a silver Audi. He was well-liked, had a nice house, good kids, a decent job. Dan had met Marie at his friend's wedding in Milton when they were partnered together in the wedding party. Second groomsman and bridesmaid. They sat together on the leather loveseat in the photographer's studio while the family portraits were being taken. Her hair was feathered back with a few sprigs of baby's breath, and the forest-green gown flattered her sporty figure. The colour had complemented her big brown eyes.

"It's awkward, I know," Dan had said, taking a sip from his glass of champagne.

Marie shrugged. "I don't even know why I'm here. I'm second cousins with her."

Dan didn't have an explanation.

"Well, you look great," Dan said.

At the time, Marie had one year left of her journalism degree but was already writing for some neighbourhood papers and smaller presses in Toronto. She made her own lunches and rode a bike to school. Marie told him how she was from a small town on the prairies and had moved to Toronto to go to university.

The day after the wedding, they hiked the trails of Rattlesnake Point. They asked a stranger to take a photo of them with the expanse of the Niagara Escarpment in the background. At the rocky look-out point, Marie stood in front of Dan and he put his arms around her waist. That night they went to see *A Fish Called Wanda* and ate Glosette raisins and drank root beer from paper cups.

Three years later, on a cold, grey Valentine's Day, they got married in the apartment they were renting on the top floor of a house in the Annex. Marie was reliable and organized, and given his own parents' dysfunctional marriage, Dan clung to the idea of commitment and stability. To the chagrin of Marie's parents, a justice of the peace officiated the ceremony, and afterward they ordered Chinese takeout. Dan's fortune read: *Follow your heart and goodness will come to you.* He still carried that yellowed piece of paper in his wallet. He made love to Marie that night and after, lay wide awake, so he got up and made himself a peanut butter sandwich, squishing the spongy bread together until it was a hard, flat, unrecognizable square. He folded the thing over and over itself, then rolled it between his palms. He chewed on the doughy ball until he could swallow it, and it sank to the bottom of his gut.

Richard took coffee beans out of the freezer and poured them like pebbles into the metal part of the grinder. He heated a small stainless steel pot of whole milk on the stove. When the kettle screamed, he poured boiling water over the freshly ground coffee, and black liquid dripped through the filter.

"The machine for espresso, it's okay," Richard said. "But you can't beat making it fresh by hand."

He winked and pushed down on the front of his kimono with his free hand.

The smell of coffee was usually one of Dan's favourites, but he was feeling queasy. Richard placed a steaming cup of coffee and milk in front of him; Dan thought he might be sick. He added two spoonfuls of sugar and continued to stir in circles even though the crystals had dissolved in an instant.

Last summer, Marie and Dan had spent three nights on Pelee Island for their twenty-third wedding anniversary. They stayed at the Seacrest, a *House and Homes* type of B&B run by a couple from Windsor, Carl and Brian, who held happy hour every night at six o'clock in the living room where guests were invited to socialize over glasses of local wines.

"I love your chardonnay," Marie said. "The Lighthouse one."

"It's not *theirs*," Dan corrected her. "She means the winery."

"Oh no, I'll take it, sweetheart," Brian shouted.

He held up the bottle.

"We order enough of this we should be part owners by now."

Carl went to the kitchen to get another tray of canapés, cucumber slices topped with cream cheese and a bit of radish.

And Richard.

"Me, I'm from Sherbrooke," Richard said, "but I live in Oakville now."

His Quebecois accent made it sound like, *High live in Hoakville*. He wore black jeans and cowboy boots. A white linen shirt showed off his sculpted forearms. Shaggy dark hair framed his face. When Brian pried about where his partner was because he had made a double booking, Richard took a glass of wine and said, "No, hit's just me."

"Okay, darling," Brian said. "It's safe to swim alone out there, but you let me know if you want someone to watch your form." He winked at him and topped up his wine glass.

The next morning, Dan took a clean T-shirt out of their red carry-on suitcase and went for a walk along the beach, leaving Marie asleep under her eye mask. He found the lighthouse. The old brick structure stood tall and dependable, facing the water, and weeds had grown over the path leading up to its door, too thick to climb through in his shorts and sandals. The lighthouse was watching, with nobody at the other end of its observations. Left to deteriorate until it eventually crumbled to the ground, it had probably been very useful once, a beacon of survival now abandoned, like an old shipwreck.

Back at the Seacrest, Richard was walking back to the B&B from his swim. He towelled off, and the two of them sat in the patio chairs on the front deck. It was one of those bright blue cloudless mornings when the moon was still visible, a three-quarter sphere, almost transparent, hanging above the lake.

"Us, we come from that," Richard said, motioning to the moon with his chin.

"How do you mean?" Dan said.

"Carbon, nitrogen, oxygen, all of it started out there."

"We are all made of stars?"

"Me, you, your wife, your kids … all of us in it together."

At happy hour that evening, Dan and Richard sat at opposite ends of the room. Carl brought out steamed edamame, red grapes, and a wedge of brie. While Marie discussed pollen allergies with the newest guests, a couple who owned a Chinese restaurant in Sarnia, Dan and Richard sipped their sauvignon blanc. Dan asked Brian about real estate on the island.

"Why is every second house for sale?"

"Mafia mostly," Carl said, putting napkins on the table.

"They do the bare minimum on the upkeep," said Brian. "But the places won't sell. Not at those prices!"

"That's a joke, *non*?" Richard asked. "Mafia?"

All of sudden, everything felt foreign to Dan. He smelled spicy chemicals—Brian's cologne, probably—and tingling sensations resonated throughout his body. Was he having a stroke? What was that checklist? Something about your face? Stick your tongue out and smile. He stuck his tongue out and smiled. He moved it to the right side of his mouth, then over to the left, just to be sure. Speech. Should he say something? Use his high school French? He whispered under his breath, "Rhubarb, rhubarb, rhubarb," just to see if he still had control of his motor senses. Richard looked at him, raised one eyebrow, then his glass. He ran the tip of his tongue along the edge before he drank. A wink. Dan looked away. His face reddened, and he held his cool glass to his cheek.

"Nobody comes right out and says it, but yes, a couple of lowlifes from Cleveland own almost everything," Brian said.

"Won't they be forced to sell?" Richard said, "By the market—"

"At a lower price, sure, but not what they're asking."

Marie was comparing ferry crossings with the Sarnians, oblivious to Dan's panic attack. It was as if Dan was looking at things through the eyes of a fly, all buggy and distorted. He forgot why he was there. What year was it? He managed to steady his breathing by focusing on the wall across from him. Brian and Carl had cut a bunch of corks in half and glued them to the wall like wallpaper. The symmetry had a sedating effect on him.

"The whole thing is a clusterfuck!" Brian laughed. "More wine?"

"We'll be long gone when the shit hits the fan, throwing back margaritas at our Mexican hacienda," said Carl.

When Dan reached for a grape from the plate on the coffee table, Richard went in at the same time, and their hands grazed each other. They each picked a grape from opposite sides of the same stem. Richard's hand was warm, and that brief connection spun Dan up again. Another wink. He was going to pass out. The rest of the room evaporated.

"*Santé*," said Richard, raising his glass to Dan.

"*Nazdarovya*!" Brian yelled. "That's Russian. We had Russian guests here once. Needed to get more Stoli shipped in!"

"*Ganbei*," said the woman from Sarnia, smiling coyly at Brian. "That's Chinese."

"Cheers," said Marie.

That toast took place sixteen months ago.

Richard and Dan had exchanged business cards when they checked out of the Seacrest, and in the fall, when everyone was settled back into schedules and routines, they became partners at a tennis club in Mississauga. They played once a week after work and sometimes on Sunday mornings. As the year progressed, so did their relationship. Weekend games became tournaments, and the tournaments became more frequent. Dan would sometimes spend the night at Richard's because of the early matches. Marie supported his efforts—he was improving his health. She said that he was in better spirits since he had lost a bit of the paunch from his mid-section.

"We should have Richard and what's-his-partner's-name over for dinner," she had said.

"James. But they split up."

"Oh, that's too bad. Well, just Richard, then."

"I'll ask," he lied.

This past summer, Dan and Richard had taken a break. Dan had not seen or spoken to Richard since the end of July. He went to movies with Marie, and they invited people over for barbecues. They had lazy and predictable sex, and he hoped she didn't notice his guilt. He watched documentaries with Sophie and trained with Hanna when she could fit him into her social calendar. Dan adored time with his kids. He enjoyed his time with Marie. He was miserable without Richard.

Dan apologized and let his coffee turn cold. He kissed Richard on the lips, and from its cage in the corner of the kitchen, Richard's parrot squawked, *"Gros bisous! Gros bisous!"* as he left the apartment.

Happy Thanksgiving.

Hanna had hoped to grab a vodka cooler from the fridge and then go out to the deck and watch the sunset alone. The sky was an amber backdrop with beams of light piercing through the clouds, casting spotlights on the trees to the west. She expected a hologram of Christ himself to fall through it all. Hanna had her school's video camera upstairs, and she knew she should go get it to take some shots of the sky and the trees before dinner. In her Can Lit class, Hanna's group was making a multimedia presentation about the themes, forms, and stylistic elements of Canadian short-story writer Alice Munro.

"How great is that," her mother had said, almost shouting.

She had been drinking since before Hanna got home from her run.

"Remember my friend Karen? From university?" her mom said.

Hanna shrugged.

"She interviewed Alice Munro for the university newspaper once."

"Really?"

"I remember that Alice said she wrote about people in her family and her town."

Her mom paused to drink more wine. Her words were slurred, but it was funny. One minute you're singing in the shower, the next minute you're drinking with your mom and talking about how Alice Munro gets her story ideas.

"But her family wasn't necessarily all that pleased about it!"

Her mom caught the edge of the fridge for balance.

Hanna took a sip from her vodka cooler. It was fruity and fizzy and didn't taste like there was any alcohol in it at all. Sheldon chased Gus through the kitchen, a sudden impromptu game of catch-me-if-you-can.

"Mrs Spada read us a piece on how Alice Munro said the thing about writing is to bring what you know *about* life *to* life."

"So you're going to write about your dear old mom then?"

"Uh, no," Hanna said. "It's multimedia. And it's supposed to be stylized, you know, like representational. Images from nature and stuff."

Her mom started to sing. "I've looked at clouds from both sides now."

"I'm going to go get the camera."

"Have you thought about filming orchids?"

"What?"

Her mother's tone changed. It was somber, almost dangerous.

"What are you going to do, Hanna?"

Marie put down her glass. Her eyes shifted back and forth like soap opera characters when things get emotional. What was she going to do when they finished this conversation? What was she going to do about the volleyball tournament next week? What was she going to do to impress the cute new media arts TA from Sheridan who was coming back to help them with their project?

"I'm going to go get the camera."

Her mom was staring at her like she was about to morph into an alien or something.

"I just want you to be okay," her mom said.

Four forty-five. Sophie and her dad should have been home by now. Her mom traced the jagged rose pattern in the crystal vase on the table. She was squinting hard to hold back tears.

"You worry too much," Hanna said.

Then her mom let out a deep groan that turned into a sigh, and she bent forward at the waist. She stood there with her body folded over, her hair touching the floor. An oval of her mom's lower back was revealed under her blue camisole. If Hanna were to ever write a story, like Alice Munro, she would have a lot of material to choose from without needing to make stuff up. Before going upstairs to get the camera, Hanna reached over and quickly patted the back of her mom's cardigan. It was really, really soft.

"A toast!" Sophie said.

"Yes," said Dan, raising his glass.

They had both been an hour late. Marie glared at Dan.

Sophie was late for everything, and Dan's excuse about traffic seemed thin. Miraculously, the turkey hadn't dried up in all that whisky.

"I am thankful for my parents," Sophie said. "For encouraging me to pursue my dreams of riding elephants in India."

Marie shifted her gaze to Sophie.

"And Hanna, sometimes you're totally self-centred and negative, but you're still a good egg."

Sophie put her glass down and wiped her eyes with her napkin. She got up and hugged Hanna first. As stiff as a tree, Hanna endured her sister's embrace and rolled her eyes.

"God. Barf," Hanna said.

Her two daughters, Yin and Yang.

"Hi, Mom," Sophie said, reaching her arms out with her head scrunched back between her shoulders.

She stood there, teary-eyed and smiling. Sophie leaned in and wrapped her arms around Marie's neck and squeezed as hard as she could. Marie smelled lavender and almonds.

"What do you mean, riding elephants in India?" Marie said.

Sophie backed away and looked at Marie.

"You look so pretty."

Was she high?

Sophie went around the table and hugged Dan just as he took a mouthful of the quinoa salad. He chewed it like he was eating marbles.

"What is this?" he said.

"It's new," Marie said. "Quinoa and celery and a maple syrup vinaigrette."

Sophie sat down and picked up the salad bowl. She put her face so close to it that some of her hair fell into the mix.

"This smells amazing."

"Dude, maybe the rest of us don't want to eat your hair," Hanna said.

"Shit," Sophie said and put the bowl down. She scooped three heaping spoonfuls onto her plate and began to eat with the serving spoon.

"It's different," Dan said.

"Different good?" Marie asked. "Or different weird?"

He shifted the food around on his plate with his fork. She took a long sip of chardonnay.

"Different good," Dan said.

"Different awesome," Sophie said between mouthfuls.

They were awesome, her family. Marie made a mental list of her favourite memories: The road trip around Cape Breton in a rented RV when they lost count of how many times they sang "This Land Is Your Land." The time Dan broke his nose trying to do a back-flip on the trampoline they bought for Hanna's ninth birthday. Their stay in a log cabin at Tobermory when Dan's mother passed away.

"I used a cool time-lapse function to shoot the clouds before," Hanna said.

"What shoot?" Dan said.

"A Can Lit thing. This guy from Sheridan is coming to do a workshop with us next week."

Marie cleared her throat. Her life was a time-lapse, a sped-up reality. Rushing around and getting nowhere. She was out of work and fantasizing about other men. And now her daughter was a drug addict.

"Nice," Dan said.

"Pass the potatoes, please," Sophie said to Hanna.

"So Richard called the other day," Dan said.

Was Dan sweating? Why was he speaking so slowly, as if English wasn't their first language?

"You haven't seen him in a while," Marie said.

Dan took a sip of wine and put his glass down. She could feel his leg jiggle under the table.

"You're shaking the whole table," Hanna said to her father.

"Right. Well … " he said.

He looked at each of them individually. Like he was taking a snapshot of their faces one by one. *Oh no.* Oh, God. He was sick. That pimple on his back wasn't a pimple after all. Cancer. It had to be cancer. Goddamnit. She'd let him tell the kids. Now was as good a time as any. He could have come to her, confided in her. There was no easy way to do something like this. No right or wrong. She felt childish for being so blasé, so complacent about him. Them. They would get through it. Treatments, chemo, counselling, whatever. Just like the time they got through the episode when he was having those late night conversations with "KimD" in the online chat room. Relationships were up and down. Marriage was a journey, not a destination. Marie would accept him as he was, her partner, lover, and friend.

"Okay, I'm just going to say it," he said.

They would get through it.

"I'm going to move out."

Sophie and Hanna looked at Marie like she should know what this was about. Marie opened her mouth to speak, but nothing came out. Nothing was moving. No one was speaking.

"Richard and I are going to get a place."

"I beg your pardon?" she heard herself say.

Dan took a deep breath and looked at the ceiling. His palms were face-down on the table beside his plate. The halogen overhead glinted off his wedding band. She had leaned back into him that day they stood against the stone wall lookout at Rattlesnake Point. Now the wall was crumbling. Cracked and broken, pieces of rock were tumbling off the sharp cliff. Falling, falling, falling into the trees below.

"What I'm trying to say is—"

"Oh my God, me too!" Sophie said.

"I'm gay," Dan said.

"It's true. I'm a lesbian," Sophie said.

Hanna ran upstairs.

"You were an hour late!" Marie said. "Both of you."

"Sophie, not now," Dan said.

"Do you think it's hereditary?" Sophie said.

"Jesus Christ, Dan. Do you even remember buying me this sweater?" Marie asked.

She repeatedly yanked at the shoulder of her cardigan, stretching it out, ruining it, but who really gave a shit? Sophie bit her teeth together in a nervous rhythm, chattering in slow motion.

"I'm sorry," Dan continued. "There was just never the right time to—"

He looked from Marie down to his plate.

Marie stood up.

"I'm going to fill up the bird feeder."

Hanna came back with the video camera.

"Wait," Dan said.

"Were you going to wait until they came out with a Hall-mark card to mark the occasion?" Marie said.

"Maybe it's part of our DNA," Sophie said, pushing back her cuticles one by one with her thumbnail.

"It would make a lot of sense. And Mom, I totally don't think you should take this personally."

Hanna fiddled with the settings on the camera while Sheldon circled around the legs of the tripod. She stood back from the table to get a wide shot. "What are you doing?" Marie asked.

"It looks like a documentary," Hanna said.

"You're pretty hot for an older woman," Sophie said. "It's totally not you."

"Let me explain," said Dan.

"I so get it, Dad," said Sophie.

"What, are you going to act it out?" Marie said. "Shall I make some popcorn?"

"It started in Pelee," he said.

She drank her entire glass of wine as if it were apple juice.

"Of course it did," said Marie.

Their conversations had become congenial and polite, bor-derline antiseptic. The infrequent and mediocre sex. His com-mitment to tennis.

"I don't think we're really that different from a lot of people," Sophie said. "I think this happens all the time."

"Sophie, please!" Marie said.

"I never planned it," Dan said. "You need to know that."

The Brussels sprouts looked like a bowl of brains. A collection of green craniums, split in half, shiny from the olive oil. The vegetables seemed bunched up in their bowl, crowded and cramped. Marie picked up a sprout and started to peel back the layers.

"You should get a close up of this, Hanna."

Hanna came over and stood behind her. She zoomed in on it. Marie picked up another one and peeled the layers away, slower this time for the camera.

"Cool," Hanna said.

When a Brussels sprout is pulled apart, you see the thing for what it is; a piece of food, sustenance. But if you peel away enough layers from the surface of an object, the thing itself disappears, and you are left with the truth.

"You should probably go," Marie said.

Sophie was picking at bits of salad left on her plate. She looked up when Marie spoke.

"I thought you might say that."

Dan stood up from the table. He went upstairs and returned with their red carry-on bag. It was already packed. Hanna had the camera on the tripod now, the lens angled at the door. Marie was blinking fast and then hard. She got up and stood behind Hanna. She put her hands on the solid shoulders of her youngest daughter. Patted down her hair. Sophie walked Dan to the door, hugged him, and went back to the dining room. Gus stood by the door and ran up the stairs when Dan opened it.

"I love you," he said to the room as a whole.

Out of habit, she began to form a mental list of things that would change: she would have the king-sized bed to herself; he wouldn't be there to complain about eating fish for dinner; the en suite would be hers. Marie went to the kitchen and found Sophie picking bits of white meat off the turkey carcass as if she had never seen food before.

"Are you high?" she asked.

Sophie looked up from the bird.

"Not anymore."

"Do you have any more weed?"

Sophie stopped chewing and nodded slowly. She went to the sink and washed her hands. Outside, the light had changed, and the sky was darkening.

"We almost named you Violet. Did I ever tell you that?"

Sophie shook her head and went upstairs. Hanna brought the tripod into the kitchen. Marie started to clear the dinner table, scraping bits of food from plates. Sophie returned with a joint, and the three of them went out to the back porch. Hanna held the camera and pointed it at the bird feeder.

"You can't shoot this," Marie said.

"I'm not," Hanna said. "And I don't want any, by the way."

"Where did you get this?" Marie asked.

"It's not what you think," Sophie said, holding in an inhalation.

"What is it that I think, exactly?"

"Like I'm some kind of drug addict or whatever."

"Are you?"

"It's Paula's dad's. He keeps it hidden."

"Doesn't he though," Marie winked.

They stood and smoked while the early autumn light faded into darkness. When they finished, Sophie sat cross-legged on the deck floor and leaned against the railing. She wanted to be alone for a minute. Marie touched her daughter's cheek and went inside. She picked up glasses and carried them to the kitchen, putting some into the dishwasher and others on the counter. Every action felt methodical and filled with purpose. Things were exactly the same but completely different. She filled the sink with hot water and added dish soap, watching the bubbles grow. At the breakfast nook, Hanna had the camera on the tripod and was adjusting the exposure.

"Seriously?" Marie said.

"It's homework."

Hanna stared into the viewfinder.

"You do look nice, Mom."

Marie went back to the table and brought the empty salad bowl to the kitchen. Maybe Sophie was right. Maybe this happens all the time. There was probably a Facebook group for people whose spouses had become gay. And what about her? She was no angel. She was obsessed with John Slattery from *Mad Men*. He was so handsome and charming and funny—all the things Dan was, or used to be. All the things except being attracted to other men. Then there was Jared, who she shouldn't be thinking about at all.

Marie plunged her hands into the soapy water, and her finger slid along something long and steely. She was hot and numb all at once. The sharp sting spread through her like an orgasm, and she resisted the impulse to take her hand out of the water. She wiggled her fingers underwater, played an imaginary harp, Tinkerbell's harp, signalling a page turn on Disney's *Peter Pan & Wendy* record that came with the storybook she used to read to the girls. When she lifted her hand out of the water, Marie saw that she had sliced her index finger along the knuckle of her right hand. A glorious gash that left blood dripping into the dishwater.

"Jesus!" Sophie said, standing behind her now. She grabbed some paper towels and wrapped them around Marie's finger.

"Do you think you'll need stitches?"

"It's not that bad," Marie said.

Hanna was still filming. When Marie waved to the camera like the queen with her paper towel mitten, Hanna stopped recording and took the camera up to her room. Sheldon followed her up the stairs.

Sophie made Marie sit down in the breakfast nook. She mentally noted the things she had accomplished. She had worked as an *au pair* in her twenties, she had seen Peter Gabriel live, she'd seen *Cats* on Broadway.

"Why don't you put some music on," Marie said.

Sophie hooked her iPod up to the stereo and a strange, looming beat filled the room.

"MC Solaar," Sophie said. "*Le Belle et le Bad Boy.*"

"How apropos," Marie said.

It was repetitive, almost monotonous, but it had a good rhythm. Marie was surprised at how much she liked it.

"The context is stronger than the concept," Sophie sang along in English.

The music got faster. A synthesizer repeated the melody over and over and over. Through the window, a streetlamp loomed fluorescent on their quiet street like a beacon on a lighthouse, the evening alight with urban glow.

Hanna brought three dessert plates and the pecan pie that had been warming in the oven over to the breakfast nook. Sophie was dancing around the kitchen, and when the song finished, she hit play again. Hanna put down forks for Marie and her sister. She slid into the nook on the bench across from Marie. Gus was at their feet, waiting. Hoping.

"It's still pretty hot," Hanna said.

Marie didn't cut the pie into slices. There had been enough carving and slicing for one night. She stabbed the centre of the pie and scooped out a gooey forkful. The girls did the same. Normally—traditionally—Marie made a homemade pie, but this year, she'd bought a pie from Carluke's. One more way to challenge old habits. Marie put her elbow on the table to elevate her wound, and the throbbing of her hand radiated straight into her heart.

And just like that, they were three women.

BROTHERHOOD

Astrid dabbed pink lip gloss on her lips and pressed them together. She checked her application in the rear-view mirror before getting out of the car. It was a perfect August afternoon in the Niagara Peninsula, and she had driven out to Brent's place because they were taking her car to Niagara Falls later. She had been to the city only once before, in the spring, when she took a trip there by herself to see the area that was the setting of one of her favourite Canadian novels, *The Day the Falls Stood Still*. Although it was a tacky tourist trap, she was drawn to the place. She never tired of the loud rushing water and clouds of mist floating above the enormous falls. Brent had made a reservation at the Brazilian steakhouse and she was looking forward to their date.

She shut the car door without locking it and smoothed out her flowered sundress. No one locked anything out here. Brent lived on a small property ten minutes outside of Port Colborne on a secluded country road off Highway 3. It was such a nice day that she half expected Brent to be sitting outside on the slab of concrete beside the house that doubled as a patio. She thought he might be out here, shirtless, in his reclining lawn chair, drinking a beer, soaking up the sun. She walked up the cement steps and rapped on the frame of the screen door, *rat-tatta-tat-tat*.

"Hulloooo," she called in her sing-song accent and entered the kitchen.

The blinds were drawn, and Brent was sitting on the floor against the wall. His knees were pulled into his chest and there was a large red mark on his forehead. It was like a breaker had blown, and all the air had been sucked out of the room. It was dark but she could still see that Brent's jeans were brown on the knees, dirty, as if he'd been gardening. His hands were filthy and his eyes were swollen and red. An empty rum bottle lay in the middle of the floor like a part of a broken sundial. There were two balls of rolled-up white tape in the corner of the room.

"What's going on?" Astrid whispered.

Brent started to sob like a child. The convulsions made his shoulders droop and shake. He kicked out one leg and slammed the heel of his boot down on the floor. Astrid put her purse on the table and went to the sink. She ran the water and placed a dishtowel under it until it was soaked through. She wrung it out, which helped steady her trembling hands. She took the towel and knelt beside him.

"What happened here to your head?"

When she placed the towel on the bruise on his forehead he grabbed her hand with both of his.

"I couldn't do it," Brent said, sobbing. "I just left him there."

"What?"

"There was a coyote in the house."

"Brent, I don't understand."

He collapsed forward, still holding onto her hand. In the dim kitchen light, he spoke through the sobs.

"Cody."

Astrid's heartbeat was racing. They were supposed to have a nice drive to Niagara Falls, pick up some fruit or sweet corn at a roadside stand, park the car, and walk up and down the side streets of the city where she would point out things—fashion, cars, architecture—that still felt foreign to her. They would pretend Brent was from Sweden too, and ask other tourists to take photographs of them. It was all planned.

"We had a plan," Brent said, letting go of her hand. The dishtowel fell to the floor. "It was a stupid pact."

In the six months Astrid and Brent had been together, she'd never seen him like this. She had never seen him so scared and disoriented. In the pit of her stomach, a dark sinking feeling formed. A flicker of selfishness passed through her, but she did not act on her impulse to grab her purse and run.

"What about Cody?" she asked.

Brent and Cody had been best friends for their entire lives. They called each other by childish nicknames most of the time— Wiz and Firefly. She was secretly jealous of their friendship. Astrid didn't have siblings and had never been that close with any friend or lover, not even her ex-fiancé, Siv. Her closest relationships had always been with characters in books.

Brent collapsed again. His head dropped forward like a stone, and Astrid felt suddenly chilled. She was nauseous, so she stood up and took a deep breath. She put her hands on her hips,

"You must explain what has happened, *ja*?" she said, commanding him, her Swedish lilt increasing along with her frustration.

Months ago, Astrid had politely declined Cody's offer after their one dinner date, if it could be called that. But she knew he still had a thing for her. She suspected it would be awkward between them when she got together with Brent but had hoped that they could work it out. It seemed that things had been improving between Cody and his girlfriend Sheila, especially now that Sheila was pregnant. Astrid had very much wanted to find a way for all of them to be friends. But as Astrid and Brent got more serious, Cody became more distant.

There was a clamour outside in the back yard by the garage. Probably that stray dog getting into the bins again. Had he said coyote? She pursed her lips, looked around the kitchen for more clues.

"Why are your pants dirty?"

Brent looked up and stared into her face.

"Where is Cody?" she shouted.

"I tried but I couldn't. He's not dead."

"Dead? What kind of pact is this? What does it even mean?"

She felt as if she was drowning. Her mind started to spin. A flash of her old kitchen in the apartment she shared with Siv in Jönköping. She kept it spotless and decorated in blue and white. Everything neat and orderly, with no trace of conflict. Brent held the sides of his head with both hands. He shook his head back and forth like he was trying to undo whatever it was that had been done. She had a profound desire to do the same thing but instead stood still, towering over him.

"Where is he? You say you know where he is?"

"Yes."

"Then we go," she turned and snatched her purse from the table. "Now!" The screen door slamming shut behind her.

Brent paced. The kitchen wasn't big enough, so he went to the hallway. Not enough space anywhere. He unravelled the white tape from his knuckles like it was on fire, and quickly balled it up and threw it at the floor. He went outside. It had been a hot, dry summer. Walking the length of the dusty driveway to the gravel road, he kicked at the ground with the heel of his work boot, picked up a handful of dirt, and threw it down. He dropped to his knees and stones poked into his skin through his jeans. The rocks were too small to tear through the fabric, so he ground his knees into the pebbles, back and forth, back and forth. Brent stood and walked back to the house. There was no more pot. He went outside again and this time, lay down in the middle of the road. It was windier than it was earlier. Clouds were moving at a good pace now, wiping the slate clear. A bright blue sky as if nothing had happened. He reached out to his sides with his arms and spread his legs. Dirt angel.

At two o'clock, Brent decided to have a drink and mixed himself a rum and Coke in one of the highball glasses he got for free when he had filled up his truck at the Petro-Canada. He added more rum than Coke. From the freezer, he took the single ice cube that was left in the cracked tray. The dog that had been hanging around was snuffling through the garbage can in the yard. Brent went to the back door with his drink and whistled for the dog to come. It climbed the cement steps, its tail swaying side to side. It looked hungry. The dog stood on the rough straw mat, waiting. Brent gulped back his drink like it was water, the alcohol searing his belly. No wonder he was drinking. No wonder he felt sick. No wonder he couldn't go through with it.

The dog had dark brown eyes that looked wild and tame all at once. It looked like a cross between a fox and a coyote, ratty orange-grey fur and a pointy nose. Brent let the dog inside.

"I tried," Brent said to the dog. "I tried, you know?"

The dog lay down and rested its chin on the linoleum. All it wanted was a nice fatty pork chop. It wanted something to eat, then it would carry on. That's right. Just get up tomorrow and carry on. Go to work and eat and shit and fuck and sleep like nothing had changed. Carry on like nothing happened.

Brent sat down on the floor next to the dog. He leaned back against the cupboard that contained a few cans of tuna, powdered orange crystals, and a plastic jug of canola oil. Carry on. Brent raised his drink to the dog and drained it. He belched.

"Let's feast!" he said. "How about some sausages from the freezer, hey, boy?"

The dog's ears perked up. It stood. Brent didn't want to touch the dog. Didn't want to touch anything. He shook out his right hand like he was trying to get water off it. He got up and took three big swallows of rum straight from the bottle. His hands had been wrapped around Cody's neck. The old rope, yellow and prickly. Dirt and leaves sloshing around in the water that had collected in the bottom of the boat.

"I did the best I could," he told the dog.

The dog tilted its head to the left. Let out a short whimper.

Brent gripped the edge of the counter until his knuckles turned white. He leaned forward and put his forehead down. He lifted his head then let it fall. Bone met hard surface. He did it again. His head almost bounced off the laminate. He could feel a bruise forming but carried on. His mind was jammed with images of floating circles and flashing white spots. Smoke rose up inside his chest. Thud. He gave over to the darkness. Thud. His legs buckled. He pulled himself up to the counter and opened his eyes, hoping the white spots would go away. He wanted the dog to stay, and he wanted it to go. He stopped bashing his head on the counter. He'd go and play some pool at The Paddock. There was a good chance Troy and Matt would be there. Ellen could make him a nice tall rum and Coke with lots of ice and a lime. Brent leaned over the sink and splashed his face with water. He covered his face with his hands. Pulled the skin under his eyes down with his fingertips. Maybe his eyeballs would fall out into the sink, and he'd wash them down the drain with more water. He dug his dirty fingernails into his cheeks and slowly, slowly scraped them down the sides of his face. The dog's eyes had turned yellow. Tiny pupils hardly even there. Its lip curled up to reveal grey teeth and black gums. There was foam and drool dripping onto the floor. It wasn't a dog. It was a fucking coyote. He'd let a rabid coyote in the house! Brent stood as tall as he could and clapped his hands.

"You tell me, boy!" Brent said. "Now what?"

The coyote snarled. A low growl curdled in the back of its throat. Brent inched his way to the cutlery drawer. He reached over with his right hand, and the coyote snarled again. A visceral, awful sound. The coyote paced. Slow and steady, it used the length of the kitchen. Brent made a monster face by stretching his face wide and lifting his eyebrows, eyes popped open like a surprised clown. He bared his own yellow teeth at the beast. Cody's eyes had been as wide as the moon. Brent growled at the coyote; he sounded like a dirt-bike engine revving up. Then he barked. The sounds came out in short, panicky yips. He kicked the screen door open with his boot. Screamed at the coyote so loud it burned the back of his throat. The coyote ran out and the door slammed shut like a shot. Brent leaned forward, palms on the thighs of his jeans. He dropped to his knees, crying like a child, his wet face a contorted, grotesque mask. His shoulders shook from the sobbing. With his dirty hands, he rubbed his eyes until they burned. He pushed the heels of his hands into his eye sockets until he saw bright orange and black, orange and black, black, orange. Black. He failed. He didn't break Cody's neck like they had planned. No burlap sack. No rocks.

Outside, a car pulled into the driveway, dust rolling up behind it. The engine shut off. A door closed. Inside, the kitchen sounds were amplified. The hum of the refrigerator, the ticking clock, the pounding of his own heartbeat. He drank the last of the rum and hurled the empty bottle at the clock. He missed. The bottle bounced off the wall, landed on the floor, and spun to a stop. It didn't break.

When Cody came to, he was looking sideways at the world. He was lying on the grassy bank that led down to the bay where the beach was flat and rocky and full of zebra mussel shells. A dandelion stood inches from his face, poking its tough stem through some other weeds. There was water running, birds, cars on a road above the bank—every sound feathery and light. When he tried to swallow, it was as if his throat had been shredded from the inside out. His breathing was short. Wiz gave it his best shot.

The dandelion, past its prime, was a perfect transparent globe. It was difficult to focus, but behind the weed was a spindly tree in the shape of a cross. Like the cross that stood in the cemetery at the head of his brother Joseph's grave. A gust of wind swept over him, and the dandelion was broken, its seeds lifting into the sun.

How long had he been unconscious? Half an hour? Half a day? Cody tried to lift his head, but his neck muscles wouldn't support the effort. Everything was wet. He coughed and a ball of jelly rose up at the back of his throat. It tasted like liver. He spat and a gloopy mess ran down the side of his cheek onto the ground. He should have just asked Wiz to shoot him with the hunting rifle.

Cody was beyond thirsty. He pulled at a clump of weeds, shook off the soil, and put it in his mouth. He chewed on the roots and they tasted like cucumber. Bits of dirt were gritty against his teeth. When he attempted to swallow, a web of fire ignited the back of his throat. Everything was tight and restricted. Worst idea ever! He seized up from the pain. He'd been in fistfights before, had the wind knocked out of him playing soccer. That was peanuts.

He couldn't focus. Squiggly dark outlines floated past the trees. He followed the half circles and uneven lines that disappeared from his vision. Random shapes. Images of random people drifting into the sky. Wiz. Astrid. Joseph. Mom. Sheila. Cody opened his jaw, attempted a yawn to pop his ears. Then he was gone again, fallen into black.

Brent had been doing pull-ups all morning on the iron bar behind the garage, and before leaving the house he smoked a joint and wrapped up his wrists with tape, like a boxer's. He rehearsed what he was going to say: Careful what you wish for, Firefly. You asked for this.

They had taken Brent's aluminum fishing boat out onto the lake. Circled back to the bay where they had always skipped stones. Brent dropped the anchor a hundred feet from shore, the ivory birches their only witnesses. It was noon, the sun was high, the sky striped with ribbed clouds. A giant tanker hauling freight was far out on the lake, a caterpillar creeping along the horizon.

Cody said, "I need this, Wiz."

They had discussed it for weeks, maybe even months—the insanity and illegality of the plan, the explanation, the cops, the evidence. The reasons not to do it. The pact. Cody kept saying over and over how he couldn't live with himself anymore. He was done. The guilt about Joseph, his heartbreak over Astrid, the shame he woke up with every day. Hardly a breeze on the lake. The boat was barely moving, only a slight rocking on the water. He tied Cody's hands and feet together like a calf's at a rodeo. He should have gone to Canadian Tire and got new twine. The rope was bristly against his hands as he wove figure eights in and out of Cody's legs, each end secured with a sailor's knot.

"You're a good—"

In one motion, Brent stuffed a sport sock deep into Cody's mouth and straddled him. Cody's eyes widened. Brent placed his thumbs together just below Cody's Adam's apple. Cody's eyes closed. His lashes were long, like a girl's, against his tanned face. His black hair was windswept and messy from driving with the windows down. Brent gripped his best friend's neck like it was any other thing: a basketball, a can of paint, a plastic patio chair. He positioned his hands as if he was about to pop a cork and pressed his fingers against Cody's throat. Not even a groan from behind the sock. The boat floated in the current's natural flow. The sunlight glinted on the surface of the water and looked like a bag of new screws scattered over concrete. It was like some kind of backwards ritual. The opposite of a baptism. Brent applied pressure, and Cody wriggled his feet at the bottom of the boat. He pressed harder. A breeze wafted through the birches as if to say, *watching, watching.*

"I'm trying," Brent said softly under his breath. "I got this."

Now he didn't want to say the things he had rehearsed.

He increased the pressure and felt a crack under his thumb. Cody's body lurched toward his own. The knotted rope held tight around his ankles, wrists. A sudden shock penetrated Brent's body. The adrenaline made him stronger. Their movement rocked the boat, and water sloshed against the sides. Cody tried to speak, but Brent spoke instead.

"You want me to stop?"

He didn't let up. Cody's body shook underneath him, but Brent was paralyzed. He felt a crumbling sensation beneath his fingers, cartilage crushing, bone breaking. Brent looked up and stared at the sun. Blinded, he turned back to Cody. Everything was white. He blinked until the white became blue and the blue became Cody, and Cody's eyes were open, glazed over with a thin, milky veil. Once Brent had seen a stray cat with eyes like that. The thing was sick and blind and let out a horrible pathetic mewl.

"This is what you wanted," Brent said quietly.

A flock of Canada geese came in for a landing. They flew so close overhead that Brent felt the rush of air from their wings. The birds glided onto the water, landing one after the other, a uniform wake behind each one.

Cody lifted his torso and arched his back. He shook his head from side to side, flailing like a fish out of water. He let out muffled sounds behind the sock that Brent couldn't make out. Maybe it was: "Wiz, stop. No." But Brent kept his fingers locked around Cody's throat. In the brotherhood, you didn't back out. They'd sealed the deal in the shed at the back of the garden when they were kids, then talked it through in the bar last month. It was sorted. It was a pact.

From the corner of his eye, Brent saw a silver flash leap from the water. He turned to look, and rings of water dissipated outward in circles. When the ripples met the side of the boat, Cody's shuddering body went slack.

It had started off like any other morning. Cody scooped blobs of Cheez Whiz onto his toast and Simon slurped sugar-coated puffed corn cereal that had gone soggy in his bowl. Simon read a Scotiabank pamphlet and ate with a child's rubber spoon.

"What are you doing with that baby spoon?" Cody said. "You're six years old."

"What is 'invest'?" Simon asked.

"Where'd you get that?"

"The table."

"You got books to read, don't you?"

"I don't know."

Simon shrugged and put the spoon down. He drank the milk from his cereal bowl then filled his cheeks with cereal until they looked like balloons. Sheila must have left the pamphlet there. She was going to ask him about opening up a joint account again. Soon she'd need baby food and diapers, and new running shoes for Simon, whose old ones had holes in the tops where his big toe pushed through the mesh.

"For Christ's sake, can't you eat like a normal fucking kid?"

When Cody was five years old and his little brother Joseph was two, his mom had left them home alone one night when she went on a date. And under Cody's five-year-old supervision, Joseph drowned in the bathtub. His mother never used the words "fault" or "accused" with Cody. She never blamed him for what happened, and she never admitted that she was at fault. It was always "the accident." And after a few years, Cody was convinced that she had completely forgotten that Joseph had ever lived.

When he was young, she would go away for days at a time

and never say exactly where she was going, only that she was "taking care of business." She told Cody that it was good for him to be by himself. She told him he needed to learn to be independent and he shouldn't count on people because they'd only let him down. He imagined she went to the city to look for a new apartment so they didn't have to stay in the house where Joseph had died. When she came back, she was always tired and wanted to sleep. She smelled like alcohol, and her hair was sticky with too much hairspray. When she remembered, she would bring him Pixy Stix. He would eat one right away and hide the others under his bed for the next time she left.

Once when she left, he ate Corn Flakes for two days straight, and when the cereal was gone he ate a box of raw spaghetti. He couldn't shit, and he had a stomach ache so bad it kept him in bed. He didn't go to school. But Wiz eventually came by with his mom, and they drove him back to their place where she fed him pea soup and crackers. She gave Cody a piece of angel food cake as big as a shoe, with pink and blue flecks in it. He could have eaten four more pieces of that cake, but was too afraid to ask for seconds.

Cody finished his toast. Simon had milk dripping down his chin. Cody went to the sink and tossed the dishcloth on the table.

"Clean your face. You look like a bum," Cody said.

Cody opened the fridge and found one tall can of Canadian hiding behind the ketchup. He reached to get it and knocked a margarine container onto the floor. It landed on its side and the lid came off. Green beans and carrots rolled out.

"Fuck!" Cody said. "What the fuck is this?"

"Leftovers," Simon said into the dishcloth.

Cody cracked the beer and drank. He worked the metal tab on the can back and forth until it came off. Ran the sharp edge up the inside of his forearm. Paused and etched another line back down to his wrist. Then a short one across in the middle, joining the two, making an "A." He retraced the three lines, harder. Blood appeared on the surface of his skin, ragged and blotchy.

"What are you doing?"

"Giving myself a tattoo. You want one?"

"Does it hurt?"

Cody wiped the tab with the dishcloth and took Simon's arm. He poked it with a short, sharp move.

"Oww!"

"Not so tough, are you, kid?"

Simon rubbed his arm and sat back in his chair.

"Maybe you'll be braver when you're older."

Cody pressed the dishcloth to his bloody arm, took a swig of beer.

"Do you want me to hold the pan?" Simon said.

"What?"

"When I help Mom sweep, she lets me hold the pan."

Whenever he spent time with Simon, he got a sickening feeling in his gut. Bits of vegetable stuck to the bottom of his boot when he walked to the door. He kicked it open and went outside to have a smoke

"Get the broom yourself. You gotta grow up sometime."

When his mom went away, Cody would wear the same clothes to school everyday. Grey rings formed on his socks around the tops of his sneakers.

"You smell like pee," the girls said.

He couldn't always hold it. He would fold up sheets of toilet paper in the school bathroom and put them down the front of his pants to soak it up in case a little bit came out. The paper was rough and gave him a rash. He turned his underwear inside out every second day because it helped with the smell. After dark, he would hang them from the waistband on the latch that kept his bedroom window open. Then he'd crawl into bed and lie on his stomach. He'd rock himself to sleep by hooking one toe over the mattress and moving it up and down.

The roof in Sheila's living room had had a leak in it all winter. Any time it snowed, she duct-taped rags to the ceiling and put a bucket on the floor to catch the water when the rags soaked through. After the eighth call to the landlord, Cody was sent to fix the roof. It took him four days to repair the damage and redo the ceiling. On the last day, she asked him to have supper with her and Simon to celebrate the completion of the job. That was three years ago.

Sheila always wore an apron spotted with red and yellow flowers when she cooked. It was an old lady kind of thing to do for someone her age. She was always doing dishes or stuffing envelopes, and the skin on her hands was rough and cracked like low-grade sandpaper. In bed, when she would rub his naked shoulders, it was like a construction worker massaging him.

"You need to use hand cream, woman."

"I use the cooking oil."

"Why would you do that?"

"I keep forgetting to buy some."

"I'll take care of it."

But Cody forgot about her hand cream and spent his entire paycheque at The Paddock with Troy and Matt and Wiz instead.

Last month, he came home from a job fixing the eaves at the elementary school and took a can of beer into the living room to relax. Sheila was there, stuffing her envelopes in front of the TV, watching *The Notebook* again. She always cried at the part where the main characters started to kiss in the rain. This was Cody's cue to go to the kitchen and make himself a fried bologna sandwich. Sheila cried at the movie. She cried in the bathtub. She cried folding laundry. Maybe it was because she was pregnant, but she even cried doing the dishes. Wiped her face with the dishrag.

When he went back into the living room with his sandwich, Sheila had turned the movie off and was sitting on the couch looking at a piece of paper with Simon.

"Here, Mama, I made you this."

For Mother's Day, he'd drawn a picture of a sailboat with a yellow sun up in the corner and black seagulls flying all around. Some grey marks were in the water, under the boat.

"What're those supposed to be?" Cody asked.

"Guppies."

Sheila took the drawing and stuck it on the fridge with a magnet and dried her eyes with the edge of her stupid apron.

"There's no guppies in the lake," Cody said to Simon.

Cody didn't want the baby. He told her as much. He told her he didn't need another kid to remind him of what he'd done. He'd asked her to get an abortion, but it was too late. Like he needed another mouth to feed, like he wanted to give this kid a life while Joseph was dead in a graveyard.

Cody followed Sheila into the kitchen.

"Can you ease up on him, please?" Sheila said.

"I'm not telling him nothing he shouldn't already know," Cody said. "Ain't no guppies in Lake Erie."

Cody took a long swig of beer.

"Minnows, now that's another thing."

"So tell him that."

"Don't tell me what to say."

Another time, when he came home from work, Simon and Sheila were sitting at the kitchen table reading the Food Basics flyer. Sheila wiped her eyes with her sleeve when she saw him.

"Fish sticks three ninety-nine!" Simon said. He pointed at the fish and kicked his legs against the table leg. Simon grinned slightly, imitating the photo of Captain Highliner on the box.

"Three three three, ninety ninety-nine," he chanted. "Can we get some, Mama? Pleeeease?"

Cody looked at him.

"Bologna and mustard not good enough for you?"

Simon slouched and sat on his hands. Sheila put her hand on his shoulder.

"You spoil him like that and he'll never stop asking for things."

"But we have fish sticks sometimes," Simon said.

"Don't sass me, boy!"

Sheila gently squeezed his shoulder.

"It's a good price," she said. "I'll pick some up when I go shopping."

Simon's eyes widened and he made the motion of applauding but didn't make any noise.

"Don't look at me when he wants a new car," Cody said.

"I don't want a car. I have a bike."

Goddamn brat always had to have the last word. Cody went upstairs to take a shower. He pulled the plastic curtain closed and let the water hit his face. Two more days to go at the library, and if he worked slowly enough, he might be able to stretch it out into three, maybe four. He squirted Head & Shoulders into his palm and lathered up.

Astrid wasn't even the kind of woman he would normally go for, but he'd never met anyone from Sweden before, and it was like she had put him under a spell or something. She wasn't big, not fat, just really tall. She was the kind of woman who could take care of things. She'd grown up on a farm, and she had perfect lips that she kept shiny pink all the time.

Cody rubbed the bar of soap across his chest, his armpits, his stomach. He washed his crooked penis, tugged at it a couple of times. Who knows what flashes before you right before dying? Maybe it was all just black, or a bright white light, or a long tunnel where you can't see all the way to the end. He squeezed the base of his dick with his left hand and jerked off with his right. He let his mouth fill with water then spit it out in a stream against the tiled wall, imagining he was shooting down the middle of Astrid's long, beautiful back.

She had arrived in January and came into The Paddock one Saturday afternoon while he was playing pool with the guys. The place was full; it was right after the area had been hit with an ice storm, and a lot of residents, including Astrid, were left without power. The bar had its own generator. Astrid looked different than the rest of them. Her skin had that rosy glow that skiers have, and she wore a thick woollen sweater that looked handmade. She ordered a white wine spritzer and sat at the bar talking to Ellen, the barmaid. When Ellen brought a fresh pitcher over to Cody and the guys at the pool table, Cody asked her about the tall, good-looking stranger. Ellen told them she was working at the library as part of some kind of job-swap thing. Port's librarian had gone to some town in Sweden, and Astrid had come here. They had even switched houses; Astrid was living over on Clare Avenue.

The next week, Cody stopped in at the library on his lunch break. He parked a few blocks up from the building, which faced the canal. He'd brought her a gift—the sculpture that Sheila had bought Simon at the Ontario Royal Winter Fair, a ceramic racehorse figurine with a shiny, glazed finish.

"How did you know to bring this?" she asked.

"What?" Cody said.

"Did someone tell you I used to have horses?"

"I just thought maybe you'd like it."

She said it was very thoughtful and he asked her out for supper, omitting the fact that he lived with Sheila and Simon.

He took her to Drifter's for wings, and at the end of the evening Astrid told him that she was flattered but she was not looking for a relationship. She was polite but firm and said that he could drop by the library anytime. Because of her accent, everything she said sounded interesting and almost made up. Even though she had turned him down, he had it in his head that there was still a chance. She could be the person to turn things around for him.

Spring came, and with it his infatuation for Astrid blossomed. He couldn't let it go. Some days he would eat his lunch sitting in his truck outside the library on King Street. She rode a bicycle around town, and there were days when he followed her until she stopped to do an errand. Once, he had timed it so they ended up at the liquor store at the same time. An interaction like that would keep him on a high for days. He told Brent how he couldn't shake his feelings for her. Brent didn't say anything one way or the other. Cody said he imagined going back to Sweden with her, putting his past behind him. He told Brent he was going to suggest it to her. For sure he could get work in Sweden, they had lots of roofs there, and in a place like that, someplace completely new and different, with no history haunting his dreams or lurking in his brain, he could be a much better person. He could be happy.

The day he decided to tell her, he bought a bouquet of white daisies at the Petro-Canada and put on an extra dab of Polo. He parked his truck in front of the library and went inside. He would tell her the kind of guy he was, a good guy. She needed to see that. She needed to see how they were supposed to end up together. If Cody knew anything in his life it was this. Deep down, deep in his heart, he knew she was the answer. So when he walked to the back of the library to where she had her work station and found her perched on the edge of her desk with a man standing very close to her, he stopped short and had to catch his breath. He ducked behind the door, and from that distance couldn't make out what either of them were saying. All he could hear was mumbling, then laughter. When he peeked around the doorframe, the man turned his face to the side; Cody could clearly see the profile of his best friend. They were looking into each other's eyes when Brent placed a hand on Astrid's cheek, leaned in, and kissed her on her shiny lips.

Finding the ad online for the librarian job exchange was serendipitous. If she stayed in Jönköping after what had happened, she would eventually confess to Siv about the affair. Things had not been great between them, and a presence lingered when they were together, an unspoken dialogue. Neither of them was making the first move to admit they had become complacent, dispassionate. Safe.

Siv ran a greenhouse that specialized in herbs and a variety of lettuces that he supplied to local restaurants. If he wasn't at the greenhouse surveying the operation, he was delivering the produce in his little Volvo station wagon that had a magnetic sign stuck on each side that read Örter från Holmberg (Holmberg's Herbs). It was a small but lucrative business that suited his reserved nature. The company became popular, trendy even, thanks to a couple of favourable articles in a prominent gastronomy magazine.

Astrid too was a quiet person who kept to herself and didn't have a lot of friends. She preferred not to make a fuss over birthdays and holidays. She loved the library, which was reserved and organized, a place where she could find drama and intrigue in the confines of the books that surrounded her. The more Siv's business took off, the more Astrid read. She stopped cooking dinner—Siv was never home anyway—and would eat in cafés alone, reading. She would spend her weekends tucked up in the bay window of their apartment with a knitted quilt and read a 300-page novel in one sitting, only pausing to make more tea. She felt deeper connections with the characters in books than with the people in her life—Siv, her parents, colleagues at the library.

From their apartment, she could hear the neighbours' music playing, easy listening and romantic. When she saw them on the street, greeting one another or saying goodbye, they looked enamoured with each other. Astrid imagined them making love all over their apartment, day and night. Her sex life with Siv had been waning; she even suspected that he had been having an affair, perhaps with someone in Gothenberg, because he always put a little extra effort into his appearance before going on his weekly delivery trips. A freshly ironed shirt, mouthwash, a shoe shine. The worst part was that the thought of him being unfaithful didn't even bother her.

When Astrid was younger, she had gone through a brief Jackie Collins phase, a secret she never told anyone. She even toyed with the idea of writing a book like that, but when it came time to put pen to paper, she found she was far too bashful to write something so racy.

She had met David at a literary festival in London. She ended up in a pub with a group of people after a day of readings and presentations. Far from home, Astrid felt daring after two shandies, masquerading as an intrepid Jackie Collins character. David ran a bookshop in Yorkshire, and they talked until the pub closed. When they discovered they were staying in the same hotel, she ended up in his room for a nightcap. None of it was planned. In the morning they said goodbye, and it was almost as if it never happened. Like a few paragraphs she might have skimmed over in an airport novel.

Once she had found the ad online, things started to fall into place. Flights to Toronto went on sale and the idea of living in Port Colborne excited her. Like Jönköping, which sat on the southern edge of Vättern, Port Colborne was located on the edge of one of the Great Lakes. It had a population of less than 20,000; Jönköping was closer to 60,000, so this would be like living in the country again. The tourism website displayed photos of Sugarloaf Marina, the town's waterfront revitalization project, and a lot of cycling and community events. Astrid took it as a good omen that Port was a thirty-minute drive from Niagara Falls. A whole new world was being presented to her like a Christmas parcel, her own private fairy tale.

She hadn't planned to meet anyone in Port. But when she had gone into the bank one day, he was behind her in the line, and they ending up having a great conversation. He was a truck driver who read books about fishing and Stephen King novels. They went on a few dates, and he made her laugh. Things were easy with Brent, simple but interesting because everything was new. Port Colborne was more beautiful and different than any place she had ever been; this move was exactly the kind of time-out from Sweden she had needed. Brent's house outside of town reminded her of the farm where she grew up. It filled her with a sense of resolution, a feeling she had been craving, a feeling that she experienced only after settling in somewhere very far from home.

Shortly after she'd arrived in Port, Astrid had gone to the local pub after a bad ice storm. Her little house had lost power, but thankfully she had a wood stove in the basement that reminded her of the old iron stove of her childhood. A strong feeling of homesickness had overcome her when she entered The Paddock that day, but it dissipated when she saw Brent. With his bearded face and plaid shirt, he looked like the images of Canadian lumberjacks she had come across in her research.

One weekend, he took her camping to Long Point where they spent the day at the beach playing in the waves of Lake Erie. The lake was so huge, it could have been a sea with its sandy beach covered, in places, with black and white shells.

"Zebra mussels," Brent told her. "Love-hate relationship with those things around here." He explained how the mussels filtered sediment from the water and made food more accessible for the bottom-feeding fish, but also made the water clearer, causing algae to grow faster. When the mussels washed up on the shore and started to rot, they stank up the beach.

"But not today," he said, and kissed her on the tip of her nose.

They dried off with beach towels and fooled around in the back seat of his car while they changed into their clothes. Then Brent drove to DJ's Roadhouse Restaurant and they had Lake Erie perch for dinner.

After dinner, back at the campsite, Brent smoked a joint and built a fire. Astrid had tried pot in her teens and found it often put her to sleep. They sat in lawn chairs drinking rum and Five Alive from plastic cups as the fire crackled and spat. Then they were quiet, entranced by flaming ribbons shooting into the night sky and a symphony of invisible crickets. Stars glittered, pinpricks of unknown worlds, and Astrid took Brent's hand in hers. Later, when they curled up on his air mattress in the tent, their bodies fit together perfectly, like a mussel in its shell.

It was Astrid's idea for them all to get together. The Exhibition was in town and there were more unfamiliar faces in The Paddock than usual on a Saturday night. The four of them— Astrid, Brent, Sheila, Cody—had been given a booth by the window. Astrid sipped a shandy that Ellen had made for her. Brent poured more beer from the pitcher into Cody's glass, then his own.

"I don't think I've ever actually sat at a table in here," Brent laughed.

"Feels weird," Cody said.

The waitress brought over their deep-fried pickles and nachos.

"Thanks, Christie," said Brent.

"I just love these," Astrid said, pointing at the breaded pickle spears. "So... unexpected."

Cody bit into a pickle that was much too hot. He rolled it around with his tongue, his mouth open, trying to cool it down.

"Hey, Firefly, those hot?" Brent said, teasing.

Cody spat the food out into the palm of his hand and took a long drink from his pint glass.

"Motherfucker."

Sheila held out a napkin so he could discard the half-eaten piece of food. He ignored her and put it on the table beside his drink.

"Back home, we pickle many things. Fish, of course, and vegetables. But who thinks to fry these like chips?"

"Who thinks to drink beer with ginger ale?" Cody said, winking at her.

At first, Brent had resisted the idea of all of them getting together. He told her Cody "had issues," and he didn't think it was a good idea. But Astrid wanted to show Cody that they could all be friends. There was nothing to be afraid of; Astrid didn't want to get in the way of his friendship with Brent. And so what if he had had a crush on her? That was in the past. He had Sheila and now a new baby on the way.

Sheila moved the straw around in her glass of orange juice and didn't say more than two words at first. She actually reminded Astrid of herself in a strange way. The thought of Sheila and Siv together in Jönköping briefly crossed Astrid's mind, the two of them tip-toeing through the greenhouse with the spray mist shooting out over the plants every four minutes like clockwork. When Astrid asked if they had thought of any names for the baby yet, Cody slipped out of the booth and put a one-dollar coin on the edge of the pool table.

"Give us a minute," Brent said.

Brent took the jug of beer and their glasses to the pool table and joined Cody.

"I like Frank, but Cody hates it." Sheila said, flattening out the crease in the napkin in front of her.

"Frank. Like, Francis." Astrid said.

"No. Like Frank."

Astrid took a sip of her drink, shifted in the leather seat.

"When I suggested Josephine, for a girl, Cody lost it. He just really threw a fit."

"But Josephine is lovely."

"Hasn't Brent told you?"

"Told me what?"

Sheila told Astrid the story about Joseph and how Cody had never forgiven himself, had a crappy relationship with his mom, and never knew his dad. Astrid put down the crispy pickle she had been holding and wiped her hands on a napkin. Cody and Brent leaned against the wall over by the pool table. She shook her head, wishing there was something she could say to Sheila.

"So, yeah. It's tough sometimes," Sheila said.

She pursed her lips and took a sip of her juice. Sheila turned to look out the window. A truck drove by, casting a shadow across her face. Sheila was plain but pretty. Her brown hair was cut short, framing her face. She wore simple earrings, pale blue beads dangling from the ends of silver hooks.

Over by the pool table, Brent had now squared off in front of Cody with his hands on his shoulders. It almost looked like they were about to get into a fight. Brent shook Cody in a firm, fatherly way, in a "get it together" way. It was a gesture of pure intimacy. Astrid couldn't make out their words, but from across the room it was as if she were watching a lovers' quarrel. Brent put his hand on Cody's cheek and gave it a couple of playful slaps. Cody smiled and they fist bumped, then Cody pushed Brent away by the shoulder. Astrid felt a pang of homesickness. She was cold. She adjusted the silk scarf around her neck and felt more like a tourist than ever.

"They're very close," Astrid said to Sheila.

"Oh, you know, the 'brotherhood.'"

Astrid did know. She wanted to belong here and fit in, but she was a visitor, an outsider. An emptiness swept through her body. Suddenly, the only place she could picture herself was back in Jönköping, sitting in the bay window of her old apartment, lost in a book.

When they were young, Cody and Wiz used to go to the Exhibition together when it came to Port for a week every August. Just the brotherhood. Now, Wiz walked around the fair grounds with Astrid, showing her off like a prize heifer.

"Cody," Simon tugged on Cody's T-shirt. "Mama said to ask you. Can I?"

The kid was as bad as a mosquito in bed at night.

"Let go of me."

"Can I play the shooting game?"

Cody reached into his jeans pocket and gave Simon a loonie and two dimes. It was all the change he had.

"Do whatever you want."

Cody left Simon at the game and walked along the path of worn-down grass in front of the stalls. He passed the water race and the birthday game, and when he spotted Wiz and Astrid, he stepped behind the ring-toss, a wall of stuffed animals concealing him from their view.

She wore the same pink sundress she'd worn to their stupid group date at The Paddock. The colour of the dress matched her lips, and her high-heeled sandals made her taller than she already was. She looked like a statue. He'd never seen such confidence in a woman. Cody's mouth went dry and he clenched his fists. Worked up a mouthful of saliva and spat on the grass. They stopped at the cotton candy wagon, and Wiz pulled off a piece of blue fluff and put it in her mouth. She touched his wrist. Cody held his own wrist. They were having so much fun. He brought a hand up to his Adam's apple and squeezed. What would it take to choke someone to death?

Simon suddenly appeared out of nowhere and startled Cody.

"Look what I won," Simon said, holding a stuffed pink and green elephant.

"Looks like a girl's toy. Way to go."

"Can I have some cotton candy please?"

"I'm out of cash."

"Please?"

"Are you deaf? I gave you everything I had."

"Hey, isn't that Brent?"

"Go find your mom."

"Aren't you going to talk to him?"

Cody pinched the back of Simon's neck with two fingers and steered him toward the entrance gate. A child's neck would break way easier than an adult's.

It wasn't the first time Sheila had called him like this. She was wearing her apron, sweeping broken glass into a dustpan on the kitchen floor.

"He's in love with your girlfriend."

Brent knew that, of course, and he felt sorry for Sheila. She was a decent person who had got herself into a bad situation.

Earlier, Cody had come home drunk and started throwing things—plates, cups, cans of food. Sheila had repotted a couple of ivy plants and he dumped them in the sink. He pulled pictures off the wall and smashed them on the floor. The glass shattered and the frames cracked. He'd had the tantrum and then walked out. It hadn't mattered so much to her before, but now, seven months pregnant, she had the baby to think about. Brent felt a brotherly responsibility toward her. When he saw the state of the place, he decided to sleep on the couch.

"What are you going to do about it?" she asked.

"What am I supposed to do about it?"

Sheila rolled her eyes and kept sweeping.

"He doesn't want this kid, you know."

One morning last week, she told Brent how Simon wouldn't eat his scrambled eggs. Cody had made Simon scrape his whole plateful into the sink. The pipes backed up, and the sink overflowed with bits of eggs and dirty water. The water overflowed onto the floor, and it took Sheila hours to clean up the mess. It was three days before they heard from the landlord who finally sent over a plumber.

"He's confused," Brent said, sitting at the kitchen table. Sheila gave him some water in a green plastic glass and sat down across from him.

"I'm scared he's going to do something to me. Or worse, Simon."

"He's not like that."

"Isn't he?"

"He's having a hard time."

"He needs help. He's always needed help."

Brent didn't have an answer for that.

"He can't get over Joseph."

"I know."

"And now Astrid," she said. "I've never seen him like this."

"Don't you think it would be better if he left?" Brent said.

"Of course."

"So?"

"I need the money."

"There are other ways."

"Not for me."

Brent looked at Sheila's swollen belly. The elastic cuffs of her grey sweatpants were tight around her ankles. Her hair needed washing.

"It's going to be okay," Brent said.

Sheila laughed. She picked up a picture from the rubble and shook it out. It had been in one of the frames on the wall, a newspaper clipping showing a colt and its mother.

"What's that?" Brent said.

"Simon likes horses so I clipped this," she said. "It was one of those nice glass frames from the dollar store."

Sheila gave it to Brent. She picked up another snapshot Cody had taken at the marina last year, before Astrid. Sheila and Simon were in profile, standing on the bridge looking out at the water. The photo was torn now and there was a big scratch across their faces.

"It's garbage," she said, handing it to Brent.

"Simon's a good kid," Brent said.

"I know that."

She scooped up the last of the ceramic shards and dirt with the dustpan and walked out to the porch, her spongy flip-flops smacking against the bottoms of her dirty feet.

"It's going to be okay," Brent said to himself.

The roof of the library had been fully prepped and he was on the final step of the installation. Cody went inside still wearing his work belt. Astrid was at her desk behind a computer screen. Her coat hung on a rack by the front door. He went over to it and sniffed at the collar. It smelled expensive. It was a light spring jacket, grey plaid with blue stripes, the opposite of Sheila's ratty brown sweater. Cody touched the slippery material. He put his hand in the pocket and pulled out a tissue and smelled it. Stale. Salty. Astrid was typing on her computer and couldn't see him from where he stood at the entrance. He pulled out the top of his pants and tucked the tissue in the front of his underwear, his penis stiffening at the touch. Astrid got up from her desk and walked down a row of books. He ducked behind a partition, holding his tool belt against his body so it wouldn't make any noise. Astrid searched the shelves, fingering the titles as she went along. At the end of the row she made a quick turn and spotted him.

"Cody?"

"Uh, yeah."

"What are you doing in here?"

She walked over and stood in front of him. He let go of his tools.

"Just checking things out from in here," he said, pointing to the ceiling.

She looked up. Her rosy perfumed skin smelled like everything good in the world. He was standing so close to her that if he wanted to he could have reached out and touched the gold chain with a heart-shaped pendant dangling from her neck. He surreptitiously touched his crotch instead, felt the tissue.

"Oh, of course," she said. "Is it finished?"

"Almost."

"Well, let me know if you need my help with anything."

She walked past him and her scent lingered. On the floor, a spider crawled out from under the bookshelf. Lost and unaware of its surroundings, it changed direction twice, then stopped in the middle of the aisle.

Sheila was asleep on her side, blankets pulled tight up under her arms. Cody tugged the covers away and lifted her nightgown. He had Astrid's tissue in one hand and slid the other hand between Sheila's legs. She sighed and straightened her bottom leg, still facing away from him, still asleep. He put the tissue in his mouth and took Sheila from behind. While the tissue softened and disintegrated, Cody pumped and pumped until there was nothing left. He pulled out and came on Sheila's leg. He swallowed. He lay on his stomach and hooked one toe over the edge of the mattress, rocking himself to sleep. Behind him, he heard Sheila getting a tissue from the box on her night table. She wiped herself before pulling the covers back up.

"You're not serious," Wiz said.

"You got a better idea?"

Brent had overdone it with the chalk on his pool cue, and bright blue powder had fallen onto the edge of the table. The tip of the cue looked like an alien penis head covered in moon dust. Brent leaned over and lined up his next shot. Hammered the purple striped ball into the corner pocket. He walked around the table. He didn't have a shot.

"You're not thinking straight."

"I'm out of options, man."

"You're fucking crazy."

"Exactly," Cody said. "And I don't want anyone else to get hurt."

"So stop being so fucking nuts."

Cody stared at him. He was breathing heavily, like a bull.

"We made a deal, Wiz."

"We were ten years old!"

Brent tried banking the cue ball off the side, then tried for the nine ball in the side pocket. He missed.

"We can make it look like an accident," Cody said. He sniffed loudly. "A burlap sack and a few rocks. Nobody needs to know."

"How does that look like an accident?"

"Okay, not an accident, but with the rocks like that, I'd never surface. No one would ever find me."

"Jesus Christ."

Cody's head was getting hot. Scratchy on top, scratchy on the inside. He rubbed his knuckles on the back of his head. He pictured Wiz and Astrid in bed together. Wiz licking every inch of her baby soft, perfect skin, sucking on her nipples with his disgusting mouth. Shoving himself inside her and her squealing like a pig. He'd seen Wiz's junk before, in the john. Average size, nothing special. Not like Cody's that curved to the right like a crowbar. Like a freak.

"It's the best thing for everyone," Cody said.

Wiz put the butt end of the pool cue on the floor. Stood there and held it like a pitchfork in the ground. He squinted at Cody.

"Is it?"

"It's the only way."

It *was* the only way. It was the only way Cody would rid himself of the guilt he'd been carrying around since he was a kid. It was the best thing for Brent and Astrid. How could Brent deny him that? Sheila would find someone better, not have to cry so much. No way was Cody going to cry. Not here in public. Wiz just stared at him, not saying anything. It was creeping Cody out. He scratched his itchy head again, scraping some skin off his scalp this time, white gunk under his nails. Wiz picked up his beer and drank what was left in the bottle in one go.

"Don't make me beg, brother," Cody said.

Wiz put the bottle down on the table so slowly and carefully that if he didn't know better Cody would have thought it was made of crystal. Wiz gripped the pool cue hard enough to break it. He took a long deep breath and shook his head. Tears welled up in his eyes.

The bridge split the difference between the good side and the bad side of Port, and as kids, the four of them would stand on the bridge, alternating sides, and watch their gobs of spit fall into the water. The gob that lasted longest got a quarter from each of the others.

Their nicknames came from fishing boats docked in the marina—Wiz and Firefly. Troy and Matt were Stormtrooper and Predator. Down at the beach, the four boys would dig through the zebra mussel shells, filling their pockets with the flattest stones they could find.

"Sixteen!" Wiz said. "Did you see that?"

"Watch this," Cody said.

He flicked the rock sideways, and as he let go it turned, hit the water straight on. Too much spin. It sunk without a trace.

"You can't even get one!" Troy said.

He and Matt laughed so hard they doubled over. When

Cody tried again and the stone skidded gracefully across the surface of the lake in six long jumps, they all had their heads down, searching for the better rocks.

Matt found a hard piece of plastic, part of a lid from a bucket, and handed it to Cody. "Flat enough for you?" Matt laughed.

"Leave him alone," Wiz said.

Cody discovered the town's public library when their grade-six class went on a field trip. When Cody got fed up, he would go by himself. Get lost in the books, the pictures, not the stories. He'd take the biggest dictionary and skip to the pages with pictures, his black curls—not from his mother—hanging down over his face as he flipped through the book. Line drawings of a boll weevil, caribou, a map of Vietnam. He'd make up stories about what he saw and tell them to his mom. He'd make up stories he thought Joseph would like.

"A boll weevil from Vietnam got so big it had to ride a caribou, all the way back to Canada," Cody would tell her.

"What are you on about?" she'd say.

He would recite stories while she put on her makeup. She curled her thin hair and applied layer after layer of lipstick before going out. She'd press her lips down on a tissue and say, "Enough of that nonsense."

If the four boys weren't down at the beach skipping stones, they were riding dirt bikes or stealing candy. Everything was a competition. Even the shoplifting. Brent and Cody would steal Dubble Bubble and jujubes from the plastic bins at the convenience store and tally up the loot in the big tire treads at the park.

"Ten jujubes," Brent said.

"I'll see your jujubes and trade you six pieces of gum," Cody said.

"That's not a fair trade."

"The gum lasts longer."

Cody unwrapped the gum and put all six pieces in his mouth at once.

"You want it now?" he said with his mouth full, pink saliva running down his chin.

"Truce!" Brent said, laughing. "Truce."

They walked back to Brent's house playing Would You Rather.

"Would you rather have a motorbike or a convertible?" Cody asked.

"Motorbike," Brent said. "A Harley and a helmet with a skull and crossbones on it." He acted out revving the engine with both hands on the handlebars, sound effects included.

"Would you rather kiss Carla Delanno or Mrs Greening?"

"No way! Neither!" Cody said.

They walked up Sugarloaf Avenue, with its well-groomed lawns and mature trees, all the way to Brent's house.

"Okay, Carla," Cody said quietly.

"You want to kiss Carla Delanno?" Brent shouted.

"Shut up!"

Cody pushed Brent into the street. The driveway was empty at Brent's house. His parents were still at work. Goober, the family collie, ran out to meet them.

"Freeze or burn to death?" Cody asked.

"What?"

"Would you rather freeze to death or burn to death?"

"Freeze, I guess."

"Not me," Cody said. "I'd rather go out in a flaming fireball."

"But you're still dead," Brent said.

"Uh, yeah. In the end, you're always dead," Cody said.

Inside, Brent got an empty Tupperware container from his mom's pantry and they took a bag of ingredients out to the storage shed at the back of the garden. They locked the door and turned on a flashlight. Cody shone the light over the container while Brent filled it with grape juice, milk, and spoonfuls of peanut butter. They sprinkled Tang crystals on top and stirred it up with an old ruler.

"Okay. So. Whatever it is, a brother just has to ask," Cody said.

"Anything?"

"Anything."

Brent nodded.

"And you have to do it. You can't chicken out."

"No chickening out."

Brent spat first, then Cody, and the white bubbles sparkled on top of the concoction. The boys waited in silence until the bubbles disappeared, then Brent stirred the mess until it was smooth. It looked like barf. Cody drank it first, Brent second. They gagged and laughed and spit some of it out. Then, hands on hearts, they swore: brothers forever.

Brent and Astrid left Brent's house on that bright August

afternoon. He got into Astrid's car, and she sped out of the driveway. He was in no shape to drive. The high from the pot he'd smoked earlier had worn off, but he was still buzzing from the rum. He was shaking. Fuck. He didn't deserve someone like Astrid. He rolled down the window and stuck his head out in the warm wind. *He* was the fuck-up, not Cody. A little Mazda hatchback passed them. Probably people on their way to the Falls like he and Astrid should be. He sat back in his seat.

"You want to know what happened?" he said.

"God help me, but, yes," she said, eyes straight ahead on the road.

He told her about the pact. Told her they swore to do anything for each other when they were ten years old in the shed behind his parents' garage. Twenty years later, Cody decided to cash in on the deal. So, that morning, Brent tried to strangle Cody and dump his body in Lake Erie. Astrid's mouth was open but no words were coming out. She was speeding.

"I didn't ask for this," Brent said.

"How can you say that!"

She'd never understand. Brent stuck his head out the window again. Fucking Firefly. Brent knew he was nuts, but this was a completely new level of crazy.

"Next left," Brent shouted into the wind, his head still outside the car.

Her eyes were on the road and she wasn't saying anything. He didn't blame her. The road didn't feel like the same road. If only he could teleport himself out of here. Fuck off to Sweden and build a new life. Or go to the Grand Canyon. It looked like a place you could really get lost in. He had seen a story about the place on the news. It was enormous. Just Brent and Astrid, living in the Grand fucking Canyon. Hiking and camping and taking pictures. Imagine that. Imagine getting away from all this.

"Stop the car," Brent said.

Astrid didn't hear him and kept driving. He opened the door and puked. She slammed on the brakes and he lurched forward, the seat belt cutting into his shoulder. He kept vomiting on the road while she pulled over.

"*För Guds skull*," she said, exasperated.

He didn't know what it meant but guessed it was something like "fucking asshole." She nudged him with a handful of tissues from the box she'd retrieved from the floor of the back seat.

"Clean your face off."

Fuck fuck fuck. Brent wiped his mouth. It was a spectacular summer day. Things looked clean and pointed. He touched his forehead and felt the bruise that had formed from bashing his head on the counter earlier. He was dizzy. He looked over at Astrid who had pulled back onto the road, hands firmly on the steering wheel at ten and two o'clock.

"Could you have done it?" he asked

"I feel like I don't know you right now."

They passed a farm on the right. Brick house with white gingerbread trim at the peak and windows. A Golden Lab lay on the lawn and there were horses behind a fence, munching on hay.

"Yes," she said, barely audible. The word landed like a rock in his stomach. "I would do it if you asked me to."

He put his hand on the door handle and was ready to pull it open and jump. Fuck it. A matter of seconds either way would have changed everything. Everything was his fault. He could have stopped it, talked Cody out of it, and helped him like a best friend should. Or he could have finished what he started.

"I just hope we're not too late," Astrid said as they rounded the curve that led to the bay.

They stopped at a four-way stop. A couple of kids were loitering at an abandoned gas station. Standing with their bikes between their legs, they looked up when Astrid stepped on the gas and squealed the tires of the car.

He wasn't dead, Cody knew that much. A primal instinct had kicked in when Cody stopped Brent before. His body overpowered his mind; he'd begged Brent to stop, and it had worked. He had wanted to die, yes, but as he lay there, the beauty around him was so fucking obvious. Geese, trees, water—he'd been living in the dark for so long that he'd missed all of this. He would find other ways to cope. Keep living for Joseph. Cody tried to swallow and it was worse than before. His throat was burning, a stinging sensation as if he was being dissected. He tasted blood.

Astrid. After all this, there was still Astrid. If he could find a way to be with her, he could get better. With her, he could straighten out. Dying was too easy. He opened his eyes just a slit and saw tiny black beetles crawling around the shells. One following the other, sinking into the depths of the zebra mussel cemetery, one by one.

The breeze was warm, but Cody felt chilled. Not dead but close to it. Maybe he could finish himself off. Fuck it. Take the easy way out. If he could get down to the water, he could drown himself. He really would be better off dead at this point, not in a beaten-up, limbo state. If he dragged himself down to the beach, he could do it. Drown himself in honour of Joseph. Yes. Death, after all. The pact would have not been a waste. He heard cars passing on the road above the bank, but he was too far down the slope to see them. It was Saturday afternoon, and there would be a lot of people out for a drive on such a beautiful day.

It was on a Saturday that Joseph died. His mom's new boyfriend had brought chocolate chip cookies and Spiderman comics for the boys. After his mom and the new guy left, Cody put Joseph in the bathtub to get him out of the way. He gave Joseph the Snoopy soap dish and a plastic fishing rod, then went and sat in front of the TV with the cookies and comics. Cody stuffed his face with cookies, the volume as high as it could go, crumbs falling on the carpet around him. He failed to notice the splashing in the tub getting louder, then eventually stopping altogether.

On the bank of the bay, an angel appeared to Cody. She rushed toward him, stumbling over the uneven shells in her heeled sandals. A statuesque creature, she knelt down and put her fingers under his jaw to take his pulse. He flinched. Behind her was his best friend, in silhouette, blocking out the sun.

Astrid pulled her car into the parking lot of the Marina. The Dutch had been doing assisted suicides since the 1980s; she'd read about this. Cody's plan was not the most orthodox method; maybe he'd read a book in which a character did something like this or saw it on TV. When Brent asked her if she could do it, she had said yes. She was able to say yes by pretending she was someone other than herself, because the one thing she could be certain of was that he would never ask her to do such a thing.

Astrid rushed to the bank where Brent left Cody and checked to see if he was breathing. A wave of relief ran through her when she found a faint pulse. But even after everything that had happened, she was still envious. She didn't understand this kind of intimacy because she had never had a relationship like theirs. Yet she was part of this. Finally, an honest experience to show her just how real things could get. The sound of the shells under her sandals was magic. The bay was perfect. She felt as if a fairy sorceress might pop out of the water at any second, a mystical Great Lake Erie princess. And there, in the water, she saw life. Something jumped and ripples dispersed, applauding the spirit within. For many, it was simply another lovely Niagara day. An ambulance was coming. Sirens were calling, and they would take Cody away. He would recover. He had a spirit too strong and too loyal to die.

Brent knelt and held Cody's hand. It was a bond she could never be part of. Hands clasped together for dear life. Brothers to the end.

Astrid closed her eyes and looked directly at the sun. She didn't belong here. There was no one to hold her hand. She picked up a handful of shells, sun-bleached and empty. Some were intact, others cracked and broken. She let them fall through her fingers and they landed on the beach, blending in with the thousands of others that surrounded them.

CHEWING SLOWER IS A SIGN OF MINDFULNESS

Val boards the Megabus with her bag of snacks and the copy of *Elle* magazine that Lisa insisted she take with her. The behemoth on wheels is full of students. Outside, it's already dark and a cold December rain is pissing down, drumming on the roof like applause. The thing is a cocoon littered with backpacks and toques and Reese's Peanut Butter cups, and in one sense, the monstrosity of the vehicle overwhelms her, but it also makes her feel like a young person again, not the tired forty-seven-year-old that she is. There are no available seats on the main level, so Val climbs the stairs and plunks her heavy purse down in an empty seat in the front row. She drapes her mauve pashmina over the window seat and slips the magazine in the mesh pocket of the short divider at the top of the stairs, the only thing separating her from the super-sized windshield. Under the blue velvet seat, she tucks the padded cooler bag that Lisa filled with far too much food for the four-hour trip back to Toronto. Val loosens the laces on her leopard print Doc Martens. She leans her head back against the headrest and closes her eyes. She presses a small metal button on the inside of the armrest. The seats recline, like airplane seats.

"Just put Frank's Hot Sauce on it, it'll be awesome," a male voice says. "I keep a big bottle in my desk drawer."

Val twists her torso in her seat, cracks her back. It looks like a game of Whac-A-Mole with their heads popping up and down in the seats like that. Where's a giant rubber hammer when you need one? She pictures going down the aisle, one by one, taking them out. Whack whack whack whack whack. She is strong enough to do it now, thanks to the yoga classes she has been going to with her daughter Molly. She can hold the plank position for a good thirty seconds.

Through the tinted windows of the bus, Kevin's old truck pulls away into the evening, and soon her baby brother will return to the eco-niche he has carved out for himself. Val is a little envious, something she would rather not admit. It had been an enlightening three days out in the country with Kevin and Lisa.

"Excuse me, is someone sitting here?"

A girl Molly's age stands in the aisle, a diamond chip nestled perfectly in the side of her nose. Her face is the colour of caramel, and her long black hair shines under the overhead lighting like in a Pantene ad.

"Go ahead," Val lifts her hand, motions to the vacant seat beside her.

"I like your manicure," the girl says.

"Oh, thanks," Val says, stretching out her fingernails for display.

Three days ago, in Toronto, before boarding the Megabus on the outbound leg of her weekend getaway, Val had gone into the drugstore next to the bus terminal and painted each of her fingernails a different colour. She waited until the salesperson was in another aisle then undid the cap on each of the bottles and applied a quick coat. Deep purple, gold, neon pink. It was a hurried job, and some polish had seeped into her cuticles. Inappropriate for someone pushing fifty, on the verge of her third divorce.

"Don't you know what's in that stuff?" Kevin had said, but Lisa had pronounced it "fun."

"I almost don't want to leave," Val says to her seatmate, who is fiddling with her smart phone. The girl pulls the white earbuds out.

"Sorry, what?"

"I was just saying how this has been a great weekend."

"Cool."

"I'm leaving my husband."

"Oh, uh... okay."

"Don't worry, it's a good thing."

The girl purses her lips and nods, which Val takes as a sign to continue.

"He tore the house apart last week," she says, shaking her head. "Literally. Anything made of paper, he ripped it to shreds."

"That's pretty... specific."

Val reaches under the seat, takes a tangerine out of the cooler bag, and offers it to the girl, who declines with a shake of her head.

"He needs things I can't give him." Val peels the tangerine in small bits, not a nice continuous strip. "Sorry, put your earplugs back in. What are you listening to? Tegan and Sara? It's my daughter's favourite."

"Lorde."

"Ah, yes," Val says, even though she has no idea who Lorde is. The girl puts the earbuds back in and turns her head to face the aisle.

It's early December, and newspapers and radio shows are ramping up for their year-in-review tributes, which has inspired Val to do the same, recording it all in her journal's morning pages. So much has happened, it seems outrageous to think that this time last year she didn't even know Clive. She takes off her purple cat's-eye glasses, hooking them into her cleavage so she won't lose them, then fishes the fuzzy blue eye mask from her purse. *Shit.* Her bangs don't even touch the top of the eye mask anymore. Why didn't she tell Lisa to stop? There was no big barber-chair reveal like on *What Not to Wear*, so when it was done, Val just stood up and went to look at her new haircut in the bathroom mirror.

"This will be much more practical for work," she told Lisa.

Annie Lennox or Judi Dench or any one of these students on the Megabus could pull off bangs this short, but it made Val look like a soccer mom who'd had a bad day at Supercuts.

On the 401, rain is coming down sideways, slapping against the windows of the gargantuan bus, drowning out some of the chatter—both on the bus and in her head. Had Clive ruined anything else since she'd been away? What was she going to say to him? Tulip was overdue for an appointment at the vet.

She lifts the eye mask and doesn't bother to put her glasses back on. Without them, the lights from the oncoming traffic are mini comets, flashes that disappear into the night. The driver turns the wipers to high, and each swipe across the enormous windshield sounds like the squawk of an angry gull. She puts the eye mask back on and wraps the pashmina around her shoulders, pulls both sides in, and makes herself as small as possible. Cocooned within a cocoon. She crosses her arms and puts her hands between her legs, sits on them as if she were in a straightjacket.

"Cross fit," Frank's Hot Sauce says, across the aisle. "How can you not know about it?"

The young man's voice is deep and slurry but not in a drunken way, and Val pictures a solid face, like a young Marlon Brando. She takes a few deep breaths from her belly, not her chest, and focuses on her diaphragm. She stretches out her face the long way, bringing her top lip over her teeth then opening her mouth as wide as it will go, an exercise she'd learned during warmups back when she was doing community theatre with the Curtain Call Players. Val had let her membership lapse but would rejoin now, show up armed and ready with the treasure chest of material she'd collected over the past year. She might even take some time off to do an acting workshop, start going to auditions again. Just the idea of it relaxes her shoulders. But she's kicking herself for not bringing earplugs for the bus trip. Val pushes her eye mask up to her cropped hairline, plucks her glasses from between her breasts, and leans forward to get a look at Frank's Hot Sauce, who doesn't look like Marlon Brando at all. He's as freckled as a nectarine, with spikey brown hair and lips too big for his face. Val imagines running a finger down his cheek to shut him up. She pictures tickling his thick pouty lips with her coloured nails and sticking a finger, maybe two, maybe her entire fist inside his mouth before he pushes her hand away and says something like, "Where'd you get that haircut, lady?"

When Clive laughed, it sounded like an empty cardboard box landing on the floor. She'd met him at one of The Flagship's open mic Thursdays last January, almost a year ago. Clive was drinking a pint of lager at the bar. Val and Trish were seated at a table nearby, drinking wine and sharing potato skins and fish tacos after their shift at St. Joseph's. The ER, where she and Trish worked, had become Val's stage, and she had started to treat her job as a nurse like performance art because it made her more enthusiastic yet gave her distance from the work itself.

"You think a bank teller has to deal with this kind of shit?" Trish said.

"I'm sure it never ends."

Val felt like there were ankle weights hanging off her, and she was tired behind her eyes. Her elbows were heavy. Her knuckles ached. She felt she should do more cardio.

Trish used a potato wedge to scoop a blob of sour cream out of a ramekin. She spoke with her mouth full.

"'Can't send them up right now because everyone is on break.' I mean, what the fuck is that?"

"The floor nurses are coming for a visit next week. It'll change things, you'll see."

"You won't see me holding my breath."

"Want to put some money on it?"

They clinked glasses. Val took a sip of wine and bit into the edge of a taco, making sure to get some lettuce. She needed to eat more vegetables, more than just the cans of V8 she carried around in her purse. Twenty-two, twenty-three, twenty-four. Val counted the number of times she chewed her food; she'd read about this in an article titled "Chewing Slower Is a Sign of Mindfulness." It recommended rolling a raisin around in your mouth for a full minute, connecting to the food you were ingesting, being mindful and aware. Anything to help with her indigestion. Only one glass of wine tonight.

Clive took his beer and moved from the bar to the red pleather stool on stage. He took a long drink then put the glass on the floor beside him and tweaked a couple of strings. He adjusted a knob at the top of the guitar, strummed a chord.

"Did you see it in A3 tonight?" Trish asked. "The leg?"

"Motorcycle accident, right?"

"Severed by a tree. Cora did the intake."

Val had been proposed to earlier tonight by a crack addict with white coat syndrome. She took a deep breath and lifted her ribcage up and to her left, then moved slightly to her right. Thirty-eight, thirty-nine, forty, and down went the masticated taco.

On stage, Clive started singing "Wonderful Tonight." He sang with his eyes closed. He was good-looking in a cuddly way, a curly brown mess of receding hair sat on top of his round face. His voice was a smooth cascade, a fountain of chocolate, and when he opened his eyes and crooned in her direction, "Do you feel all right?" She mouthed the rest of the lyrics along with him. "Yes, I feel wonderful tonight."

Drinking with Clive had been fun at first. He would play Neil Young or the Eagles while she danced around the living room in her knitted socks, each toe a different colour: orange, yellow, blue. He'd sing, "I like the way your sparkling earrings lay," and she would lean in, hands on his thighs, and circle the top of his bottle with her tongue. It always led to more, often right there in the living room. Sometimes a long slow fuck against the wall. Her Mimico bungalow became a refuge in a swarm of chaos, a private pod of tranquility.

By Valentine's Day Clive had moved into Val's place, and since neither of them were particularly interested in heart-shaped boxes of chocolates or foil helium balloons, they opted for a quiet night at home with a spaghetti dinner (his favourite) and a bottle of Prosecco. Clive had made his signature Caesar salad dressing using his mother's recipe. Wearing nothing but her apron with GRILL QUEEN! printed in flaming red letters on the front bib, he whisked away in the kitchen. He brought the dressing over to the table. She rubbed his naked butt, and he leaned down for a kiss. A kiss that turned her sideways, then upside down. A kiss that opened up possibilities of a future where there were no complications cresting and crashing around her. A kiss that suggested a future of teasing and retreating, conviction and pleasure. A kiss that lived in a place she already felt a desperate longing to hold on to, like this moment, already slipping away. Val yearned for the quixotic kiss to play out, the meeting of flesh against flesh, a sensuality tinged with experimentation with parts of her that were less obvious, desires she had kept hidden for fear of being judged, broken, or mislead. Val had been protecting herself for so long, she'd pinched off her vulnerability like a bloom gone to seed. She was nearly hyperventilating when the kiss ended and Clive dipped his finger in the bowl, then held it out for her to lick.

"It's important to get the oil and egg mixed properly. Critical, in fact," he winked.

This was the kind of man she needed in her life. Someone she could hit the pause button with. Someone centred. She was too old for running around and playing games. Here was Clive, a man who prioritized things like family and music and moments just like the one they were having now. There was something else about him she couldn't name yet, couldn't classify, but she felt a growing admiration for him and his focused dedication, which, she had assumed, included her.

"Let it sit a minute?" she said, licking her lips and lifting the apron away from his body. "It's just a dressing."

He shot her a sudden look of rancor and twisted his hips away from her.

"You're kidding, right?" He continued whisking with a renewed force, a rapid-fire approach. He was whisking like a propeller on a helicopter about to take off, the muscles on his forearms tense and bulging. "I haven't even tasted it yet."

By spring, Val started to see qualities in Clive that she would jot down as observational research. He dealt with his mother's breast cancer partially by closing up as tight as a vacuum-packed steak. Val convinced herself that taking notes on his behaviour would help her not only try to make sense of him, but could also be useful material for future acting roles. Her notebook read, "Physical traits to show anti-social behaviour: extreme object fixation such as newspaper or coffee cup, silence, lack of facial expression, unable to have direct eye contact during conversation, forced gestures (smiles, laughs), awkward and unnatural body language (embraces, hand shakes) with friends or relatives. Psychological traits: withdrawn and distant, denial of/inability to cope with parental suffering, over-reaction to small issues (e. g., empty milk carton put back in the fridge by mistake)."

A sudden May thaw revealed an abundance of garbage that had collected under snowy lawns and gutters, now on display in all its urban glory. The trash was balanced by the sprigs of life that popped out from their dormant winter sleeps, like the patch of yellow crocuses that carpeted the parkette near their house. Occasionally, if she wasn't working the night shift, Val and Clive would go for a walk in the neighbourhood after dinner, their stroll often ending up at the Albatros Pub. The streets of South Etobicoke were surprisingly quiet even though they were so close to Lake Shore Boulevard. The high sprawling limbs of mature maples reached across the roads as if to take hold of one another, their branches longing for companionship; in some cases, it was impossible to tell where one tree started and the other ended.

Once, a stray cat padded out from an alley and followed them. Clive bent down and coddled the ragged calico as if it was a long-lost friend. He scratched it behind the ears and the cat dropped to the pavement, intoxicated with pleasure.

"Look how vulnerable," Val said.

"She knows I'm not going to hurt her."

While he was crouched on the sidewalk, Clive leveraged himself so he had one knee on the ground, then pulled a navy velvet box out of his inside jacket pocket.

They had talked about getting married briefly, almost arbitrarily, because he wanted his mother, a traditional Lutheran woman with an only son, to see him wed before she died. It wasn't a big deal for Val, who had been married twice before and didn't need a ceremony to prove what he meant to her. Getting married was the least she could do for him, a guy who had brought her the peace of mind she hadn't felt in years. She couldn't imagine herself in the dating world again. Some of the younger girls at work met people online and the way they described the multiple-choice questions and surveys, the experiences sounded more like high school exams or job interviews. Val would rather chew glass.

The ring was a solitary princess-cut diamond set in an eighteen-carat yellow gold band, a seriously classy piece of jewellery, which she had not expected. Designed with a tension setting, the gem appeared to be magically held in place, suspended between the two edges of the band by nothing other than sheer will.

"I thought you could wear it to work because it's flat," he

said, taking her hand in his, and they walked like that all the way to the Albatros, the little stray cat trailing along behind them.

In June, Clive's mother took a turn for the worse while they were on a portaging weekend in Algonquin Park. Val and Clive had paddled their way along the lake through layers of green and yellow lily pads where they saw a moose and its calf wading, tucked in at the base of the tree line. They set up their tent, and Val cooked chunks of parsnips and stewing beef in a stainless steel pot on the camp stove while Clive played "Smoke on the Water," keeping time with the waves lapping the side of the embankment below.

"I can see how the Group of Seven got inspired out here," Val said.

"Who?" Clive asked, continuing to strum his guitar.

The darkness circled in around them like burglars. Loons retired for the night and crickets took their place in the grass. Crackling orange sparks from the fire shot into the dark sky, crammed with stars. It was well past midnight and they had been drinking for hours when they decided to take the cooler bag out into the bush. The nineteen-year-old with pierced eyebrows at the information kiosk whose golf shirt read DYLAN had recommended hanging their food in a tree at night.

"There've been, you know, um, bears," Dylan said.

"How many?" Clive asked.

"I don't know ... six?"

"Six!" Clive said. "It's only June."

"Yeah, um, I don't know," said Dylan. "Here's some rope."

They tramped over twigs in the dark. Val carried the coil

of rope on her shoulder while Clive carried the cooler bag and waved the flashlight around like a wand. Val tripped over a thick root and fell back and he caught her waist from behind. She turned and he pointed the flashlight up under his chin and in his best vampire voice said, "I vant to suck your blood!" Then the light flicked off. His hand was instantly behind her head. Fingers pulling her hair back and down. Like a ghost, his lips brushed the base of her neck. He kissed her jaw, her earlobes. Orion sparkled high above them and she reached out for his belt. In the dark, Val found the leather strap, tugged firmly, and the buckle released and opened.

Because of his mother's declining health, they pushed the wedding date up and got married in July. Val picked up a frilly old dress from Value Village for twenty bucks that was yellowed at the neckline, the stiff crinoline skirt a little too short. She wore white sequined flip-flops and let Molly paint her toenails lime green. The ceremony took place in their backyard, and as soon as everyone had left, Val took off the gown, stuffed it in a big black garbage bag, and shoved it behind the camping equipment in the basement.

Their wedding night was spent on Clive's buddy's boat in Bluffers Park Marina where they drank a bottle of Lanson champagne and ate chocolate-dipped strawberries out of a plastic container from Loblaws.

"Is there any more food?" Clive asked.

"I brought some hummus and pita chips," Val said, chewing on a strawberry. "And a bag of kettle corn."

"I hope Marty doesn't want me to do a job for him for using this boat."

"I thought it was a present?"

"No such thing as a free lunch, sugar," Clive said and slapped her ass.

She got in her Jetta and went to get more booze. She bought a case of Moosehead and a mickey of whisky at Clive's request, and when she returned to the boat, he parked himself in front of the flatscreen in the hull and watched the PGA tournament on satellite TV. They each had a shot of whisky and then he promptly drank ten bottles of beer, one after the other, and passed out in his tuxedo shirt. Val went up on the deck and stretched out on the vinyl cushions. She wrapped herself in a fleece blanket and wrote in her journal. With her blue glitter pen, she made a list of the ways she would be true to herself in this marriage: eat better, spend time alone, enroll in an acting class, stay until his mother passed away.

If the sky had a flavour, it would be an orange cream hard candy. The longer she looked at it, the creamier it got. Her notebook absorbed the colour of the sunset. The lake too. Pinky orange-tinted waves glittered all the way to Rochester. High above, signals flashed out of sync on the wings of an aircraft, a baritone roar echoing behind it. The jet left a scar in its wake, marring a perfectly good canvas. Val traced the faraway contrail with her finger, then lowered her hand and turned the gold band around her finger until the diamond came full circle. She tilted the stone back and forth in the dimming light and, depending on the angle, the sparkle appeared to be turning on and off, like a switch. And when the sky was drained of colour, when only the darkest of blues remained, the jet-stream scar disappeared, and none of it seemed as damaged anymore.

Outside the Megabus, rain turns to sleet, icy pellets pinging against its giant windows. Val stretches her arms to touch the console above her head. They left Kingston over an hour ago, and it feels good to move her body. The chatter has subsided, and the bus glides along like a dream-liner in the night. She wiggles her fingers, turns her wedding ring with her thumb, and reaches a little higher to turn off the overhead light.

By Thanksgiving, Val suspected that Clive had been starting to drink as soon as she left for work, so on an overcast Saturday, an hour before her ten o'clock shift, while her husband of three months lay snoring in bed, Val topped up Tulip's cat food, gave her some fresh water, and left the house wearing her scrubs and carrying a travel mug of espresso. She made for the spot in the hedges that she had scoped out two days prior where she had a clear view of the kitchen window.

Within ten minutes, Clive had taken the vodka bottle from the cupboard and poured himself a glass. He sat down at the table and stared in the direction of the fridge, talking to himself while his chin jutted forward between sentences. He shrugged his shoulders a lot and finally held them up in a raised position. Then he raised his hands up to his ears, both palms out and facing the ceiling. His body language said: How the hell should I know? He finished the drink like it was Kool-Aid and brought the empty glass down hard onto the table. Making a fist with his other hand, he slammed it on the table, then ran his hands through his hair. Clive went back to the counter for the bottle, refilled the glass, and started the whole cycle over again.

Val stuffed the empty coffee mug in her oversized purse where it clanked against a can of V8 and walked like a speed walker, arms swinging up and back, up and back. She got to the parkette in half the normal time and sat on one of the benches by the fence. With a fine-tipped fuchsia uni-ball she noted careful observations of everyone passing by: "Old man hunched over walker, worn-out shoes. Lady with short brown hair walking two Dachshunds—one dog much older than the other. Male jogger in unflattering black biking shorts and utility belt with miniature water bottles that resemble urine samples." Later she would file these pages, her research, into individual folders in the drawer of her nightstand. When she got back into theatre, she would be bursting with new characters.

Clive stayed drunk for the entire month of November. If there was a tipping point that prompted her to take the Megabus to Kingston and stay at Kevin's for the weekend, it was the paper-shredding episode. Last Friday, she had got home, after working an all-night shift, at six in the morning and found the door wide open. Had they been robbed? Had Clive left the door open all night? Tulip. *Please let her little cat be okay*. Val's breathing quickened, and a wave of heat swept through her body and made her face flush. Something was blocking the door.

It wasn't a burglar. She pushed harder against the door and moved the stacks of newspaper and cookbooks that were blocking the entrance. Sheet music everywhere. He had torn up all her notebooks and plays and files, and from the paper he'd constructed an entire cityscape. Three black hard covers, gifts from his mother, stood in the middle of it all like gravestones— *Dracula*, *The Great Gatsby*, *War and Peace*. More novels were lined up in front of the sofa like townhouses. Magazines were rolled up into towers. The construction covered the entire living room floor.

Tulip batted a small piece of paper around like a puck. Pausing when Val entered the room, the cat came over and rubbed her head against Val's shin, then turned and stalked a balled-up piece of newspaper. She climbed through brown tunnels made from liquor store bags. Crouched low, she set her sights on her target, prepped the pounce, then launched and landed in the middle of the mess. She knocked over one of the hard covers, which spooked her, but she stood her ground, tail puffed out to three times its regular size. Then she sat down and started to violently lick her left paw.

Later that same morning, Val met Molly at the Yoga Den for an Ashtanga class. Val had joined Molly at her classes in Little Portugal for the last six weeks, and the weekly gathering with strangers to collectively ease their frantic lives helped her to cope with Clive. Tea lights dotted the edge of the studio floor every two feet. It was like church, like being in a room with a congregation of blonde, pony-tailed, stretch-pant-wearing disciples, all of them desperately trying to locate their centres by lengthening and lifting, elongating and expanding. Val wore her old navy leggings that sagged at the crotch. She yanked them up and rolled the waistband over so it didn't cut into her gut as much. She was exhausted but pushed through and embraced the fatigue.

While Val was trying to press her chest toward her feet in downward dog, the instructor came over and ran his hand up the small of her back. He cooed, "Keep your core lifted. Centred," he said. "Don't let it fall."

At the end of the class they all stood in mountain pose. The svelte teacher floated around the studio like a ballerina and told them to imagine being pulled upward by an imaginary piece of string attached to the crowns of their heads. Focus. Val tried hard not to focus on what she'd left at home. The instructor came up behind her, put one hand on each shoulder, and gently pulled back two inches. It felt like two miles. She and Clive hadn't had sex since Algonquin, and it was now almost December, already three months since his mother's funeral. With the instructor's helpful touch, Val's head magically lifted and her spine elongated. Her chest opened up and she could breathe again. *Namaste*.

"Bunch of people got let go at Farukh's office last week," Molly said in the change room.

"But not him?" Val said.

"For now, yeah."

"Is he worried? Are you worried?"

"What's the point of worrying?"

Molly had it so much more together than Val did at her age. She had it more together than Val did now. Molly and Farukh were in a healthy, long-term relationship, and Val secretly hoped some advice might spill out in her direction over lunch. How did they make it look so effortless? Had she learned nothing from two failed marriages? But she wasn't going to unload on her daughter about Clive. Molly had never come right out and said it, but Val sensed her disappointment with him.

Molly rolled up her flowered yoga mat and zipped it into its carrying bag. The other women in the room did the same, every-one protecting their soft places to fall with permeable nylon shells. Val was still renting a mat for two dollars at every class. Maybe it was time to break down and commit. She wrapped her long wool sweater over her T-shirt and leggings and tied the belt in a knot at her waist. Molly had changed into a pair of brown tights and a fuchsia miniskirt. They collected their coats and scarves at the entrance and Molly leaned in toward the mirrored wall and dabbed rose-coloured gloss on her lips. Val resisted lifting a lock of her daughter's hair that was tucked into the back of her coat collar. This young woman had been a child once upon a time. Once upon a time when Val was essentially a child herself.

They went for lunch at an Asian fusion restaurant on Ossington, a few streets over. Val wanted to confess to Molly how, just last night, Clive had torn the place to shreds. She wanted to tell her daughter how backwards things had become, like a pillowcase put on inside out, seams showing all the way around. But becoming a burden to her child was the last thing she was going to do.

"It's not like I need a new job," Molly said.

Molly had asked the waitress for iced green tea, unsweet-
ened. Val ordered a Vietnamese coffee.

"I just thought I had a better chance," she said.

Molly hadn't got a call back from the ad agency where she
had applied for a position as a junior strategist.

"With my experience level, you know."

She was twenty-four.

"Opportunities come and go," Val said, taking a bobby pin
out of her hair and letting out her bangs. She pushed her hair
back and then stuck the pin back in.

"Do you want to order a few dishes and share them?" Val
asked.

"It's usually better to do that with a group."

"Oh, okay."

"And I don't eat fish anymore, remember?"

"Right, sorry."

"But yeah. Order whatever. Make sure you get the green
onion pancakes."

On the do-it-yourself menu, Val ticked off green onion pancakes, garlic shrimp, mixed vegetables with rice, and marinated
tofu. She felt like checking off one of everything on the list. She
felt like ordering a hundred dishes and sitting there with Molly
on the off-chance she might be of some use in her daughter's
life.

"The posting said: Ability to effectively coordinate multiple
projects, meet deadlines, and prioritize," Molly said. "Hello?"

"You have all of those qualities and more, my dear."

"Right?" Molly pulled her iPhone out of her purse. "Things

just aren't happening as fast as I'd hoped." Molly thumb-typed onto the keyboard, engrossed.

"Tell me about it." Val took a sip from her plastic glass of ice water. She was starting to feel light-headed, delirious. After wading through the mess of papers, Val had found Clive passed out in bed.

"I won't be in class next week because I'm going to see your Uncle Kevin and Lisa."

"You have to take some kombucha for Lisa. Did you try it yet?"

Val hadn't had a chance to get to the health food store to pick up the new fermented drink that Molly swore by.

"No, not yet."

Molly scrolled through her Twitter feed while she spoke. "I'll see you and Clive for dinner on the fifteenth, right?"

The waitress returned and set down a plate of six green onion pancakes between them. Val didn't answer so much as mumble. She took a bite from the speckled fried dough and began to count how many times she chewed.

"How is Clive, by the way?"

Val had been single for six years. Before Clive there was Allan, a beefy blond teddy bear of a man whom she had met in the ER when he'd brought in a listless captain of a football team with a broken collar bone. Allan was a high school teacher who liked astronomy and cars and working out, and they were together for eight years, most of them good. She had been in great shape during the five years they were married. The relationship ended because they simply became two people who fell out of love with each other. Before Allan there'd been Grant, the love of her life, whom she married far too young. They had that supercharged kind of first love you get in your twenties when you're fortunate enough to know everything. The kind of love that, for ten reckless, risk-fuelled years, spurred them to experiment with cocaine and threesomes and hitchhiking. When Grant finished his business degree and started to work for a multinational IT company, it was the sobering discovery that they had conflicting value systems that ended it. But they would always have Molly.

When Molly was three years old and they were living in a basement apartment in Parkdale, the three of them had picnicked in High Park on a quiet August long weekend. Val packed a cooler full of watermelon slices and potato salad and filled a thermos with ice and sparkling lemonade. The public pool was full of frolicking city dwellers without cottages. Grant rolled onto his back on the grass, bent his knees into his chest, and placed Molly on his bare feet. He held out his ropy arms and extended his legs. She giggled like a pixie and wriggled her tiny bum back and forth, and Grant let her down gently.

Four geese that looked like drunk security guards waddled over, unbalanced in their grey-brown feathered suits and pipe cleaner necks.

"Will you be my friend?" Molly asked as she offered her watermelon to a goose.

"Molly, please don't feed the birds," Val said. She tossed a slice at Grant. "Think fast."

It hit him in the chest, and he caught it against his T-shirt with one hand. He put the whole thing in his mouth and smiled wide, a dark green band covering his teeth. Molly ate her piece of melon as fast as she could, pink juice dribbling down her chin. She tried to make a smile like Grant, but her face was too small and the peel stuck out of her mouth like a kazoo. Val ate slowly, bite by bite, savouring the sweetness of summer. If a flood came and swept them away, geese and all, everything she had ever wanted was contained in that very moment.

The ER, Val had learned, doesn't discriminate. It welcomes all—homeless people, celebrities, the helpless and the powerful, both poor and wealthy. Patient profile: male, Caucasian, fifty-five years old, five-foot-nine, 150 pounds, golf shirt, khakis, loafers.

"I have a headache," he said to Val.

"For how long?"

"Two hours. I might be having a stroke!"

"Did you drink any water today?"

"I was drinking last night. How long is it going to take for me to see a doctor?"

"Six to eight hours maybe."

"I could be dead by then!"

"You probably aren't having a stroke. You might just be dehydrated from the alcohol. However, I'm not a doctor."

"That's right, you're just a nurse. I'm going to sue the hospital for this injustice."

"All right, that's fine, please have a seat. There's a water fountain down the hall, that way."

Another night, Val arrived at work to take over the evening

shift from Trish and found her standing alone in a treatment room. There was a child's body on a gurney behind her, brown hair just visible from under the sheet. Trish faced the wall, and was scratching at a bit of scotch tape with her fingernail. The five-year-old boy had been killed by a friend while they were playing with knives, unsupervised. Val placed her hand on Trish's back. Trish got the tape off the wall but kept on scratching.

"Take yourself out of it," Val said. "It's done."

Val rubbed Trish's back in small circular motions. Trish stared at the ceiling. The ER was an organism, a heaving, wheezing, laughing, screaming flawed creature, where perseverance didn't necessarily mean success or a happy ending. It was a complex system of many parts that functioned as a whole to maintain a sense of achievement, a sense that things could be fixed. The ER was an entity in which hope was too often trumped by fragility, the weak were discarded, taken away, and deleted, and strength was a scarce commodity.

"It's one reality," Val said to Trish. "One among many."

She said it out loud to convince herself as much as Trish. Val did more acting at the hospital than she'd ever done on stage. She took Trish's hand and massaged the fleshy part at the base of her thumb. The head nurse poked her face into the room. Saw the gurney. Saw them holding hands.

"Either of you two seen the McIntyre file?" she asked.

Once, an elderly man came in with pains in his chest. He'd said it was his heart. While Val checked his vitals, the old man told her that his wife had died two weeks ago.

"She was hit by a car," he said.

"I'm sorry for your loss," Val said.

"Broad daylight. At a crosswalk."

Val undid the padded Velcro wrap from his arm and hung it back up on the hook behind him. He was a fragile little fellow with thin, silky skin.

"Try and get some rest," she said. "You've been through a very emotional time."

He looked at her and tilted his head. A sparrow with a broken wing, confused, unable to fly. The old man shuffled out of the examining room but returned every night, just before midnight, for a whole week. The nurses nicknamed him Boomer, as in Boomerang. His blood pressure varied on each visit, slightly low, but nothing life-threatening.

Val had had two days off, and on her next shift she brought in a box of lemon balm tea for Boomer.

"Oh," Cora said. "No one told you."

While Val and Cora prepared an IV drip, Cora told her. "Cardiac arrest on his way out last night. Right there in the entrance."

The flimsy cardboard box of tea was still in her purse, the corners covered in plastic.

"Died of a broken heart," Val said.

Through the clear liquid of the IV bag, the room appeared blurry, distorted. The thing was an upside-down puppet, hanging out in the open with nothing to protect it.

Val thought a visit to see her brother Kevin might help resolve her feelings about Clive, make a plan, take in some of that country air for clarity. Kevin, his girlfriend Lisa, and a colt-sized Newfoundland dog named Jake lived in a mobile home forty-five minutes north of Kingston near Gould Lake. They were off-grid, with a composting toilet and a rain-catch system. They had a pond stocked with trout and a garden plot where, in the summer, they subsisted on homegrown tomatoes, eggplant, and pot. It was December, but Lisa still had parsley and basil growing in little wooden apple baskets on the kitchen counter beside the sink.

Kevin and Lisa had been together for over a decade. They'd bought this place five years ago. The house was littered with things they had found in the area—fence posts and recycled barn wood and a tree stump made into a chair. They'd turned an old door into a table and put it out on the sun porch that Kevin had built. A hibiscus plant the size of a Christmas tree stood in the living room.

"The buds are edible," Kevin said.

"We found it on the side of the road," Lisa said. "You'd be amazed what people throw out."

Lisa got up and ran her hand around Kevin's shoulders. She plucked a tightly wound red tube from the plant. "We'll put this in a salad tonight."

Like Molly and Farukh, they made it look so easy.

After they got engaged in May, Val and Clive had gone to see Kevin and Lisa. She cooked a fillet of trout that Kevin had caught that afternoon, cooked it *sous-vide* in the kitchen sink, just floating there in a baggie, and served it with a sesame-coriander sauce. It had the consistency of butter. Even Clive liked it.

"Have you seen that bacon that comes already cooked?" Clive had asked.

"That's not food," Kevin said, taking a bite of fish.

"Sure tastes like it to me."

"You're an advertiser's wet dream."

"Because I like bacon?"

"Yeah," Kevin said, nodding, "because you like bacon."

"Are you mocking me?"

"Am I mocking you?" Kevin repeated in a high voice.

Clive grabbed the bottle of vodka off the dining room table, walked out of the house, and didn't come back for an hour. They finished eating, and Lisa went to bed to read. Kevin and Val took their drinks out to the sun porch.

"What are you, twelve?" Val said.

"He was asking for it."

"You could have left it alone."

"I don't get it. You with him."

"You don't have to."

On the second evening of Val's December visit to the eco-ranch, they all had a shot of the ginger kombucha that Val had remembered to bring with her. Molly was right; Lisa was pleased with it. Kevin liked it too and had a second glass. Val thought the stuff tasted like spiced vinegar. After dinner, Lisa took Jake for a walk while Val sat in a lawn chair in the dining room sipping a glass of Kevin's blueberry gin. Kevin tossed the squash peels and red pepper stems into the vermiculture—a Rubbermaid bin in the corner of the kitchen—and gave it a stir. Then he lit a joint and sat on his tree stump.

"Your aversion to transgression is steeping in confusion," he said.

"And reeking of compassion."

"Compassion?" Kevin said. "Don't you mean submission?"

She gave him a pointed look from under her freshly cut bangs. Kevin passed her the joint, and she took a hit.

"You're not that different, you know," Val said.

"Say whaaaat?"

"Tucked away out here in your wilderness hideout." She inhaled. "Sealed off from everyone."

Kevin took a long toke and held it in. "Correct."

"You do the same thing as Clive," Val said. "Confine yourself to an extreme so you don't have to deal with reality." Val didn't say that was exactly what she'd found attractive about Clive in the first place. Singing on stage with his eyes closed, off in his own world, Clive claimed the space around him, and she wanted to do that too.

Kevin got up and poked at the logs in the stove.

"It's just choice," he said.

Val raised her glass. "To better choices, then."

The next afternoon, Val took Jake and went for a walk down by the creek at the edge of the property. Black branches tattooed the sky, and in the breeze, the leafless trees spoke their own language. The wind never disappointed her; air was her favourite element. Val knelt in the damp earth and ruffled the dog's ears. When she rubbed him under his chin, Jake's nostrils flared out and he let out a breath. The gentle beast trotted ahead of her, paused three times to sniff at the ground, and marked each stop with a piss.

Val walked with her hands in the pockets of the parka she'd borrowed from Kevin. A folded-up piece of paper was in the pocket with a note on it that read, "I love being here with you."

If only she had been able to see what she and Clive would become. If only, when she'd first seen him at the bar, she had drank her wine and chewed her tacos and left it at that. If only she could sink into the earth right here, become a watcher, a presence, like the wind. Jake came back and nudged the back of her thigh with his big head.

"Hey, buddy." The dog stood beside her, his nose facing into the wind.

"Jake," Val said and he turned.

"Sit."

She squatted on her heels in front of him, face to face. "Clive, you don't know this, but I made a promise to myself that night on the boat, our wedding night."

The dog sat listening, panting, waiting.

"I have been true to you, to this marriage, but it's over."

A small flock of starlings whipped by and Jake started to bark.

"That's right. Not an easy thing to hear, I know. Not an easy thing to do!"

Then the dog lay down in front of her, stretched out his jumbo paws, and lowered his head.

"It's what we need. You must see that."

Without lifting his head, Jake looked up at her with his sloping brow, eyes so dark and astute she thought the dog might develop the ability to speak right then and there and reply to her in plain English.

"It's okay, Jakey, it's all going to be okay. 'Cause you know what else?"

She patted both palms on her thighs to get him to get up.

"You know what else?"

He stood, shook out his black coat, and came closer to her. She smacked him gently on the rump a few times.

"I'm going to start acting again!"

She ran in a circle then, leaping and jumping like a child. Jake jumped up beside her in his lumbering gallop and uttered more slobbery barks. She picked up a branch and tossed it as far as she could, and he made a beeline for the stick, never losing sight of it for a second.

The Megabus was almost fully boarded when Kevin dropped her off at the bus terminal in Kingston. He gave her a hug in the cold rain and said, "If things don't change, they're going to stay the way they are."

A running joke between them was to see how long they could keep a conversation going and say absolutely nothing.

"Well, this is it," she replied.

"That's the thing."

"You're so right."

"Damn right I'm right!"

How solid her baby brother had become. How grounded

and focused. He gave her a Boy Scout salute and climbed into his old brown pick-up.

Three and a half hours into the trip, Val starts to feel queasy. She reclines her seat and tries not to disturb sleeping beauty beside her, who has nodded off. They are almost home. Mucky water splashes under the tires outside. The sleet is stronger now. The bus is being bombarded with frozen artillery.

The Megabus gears down.

The cooler bag at her feet contains two coconut Lara bars, three tangerines, a box of chocolate-covered almonds from a neighbour kid's fundraising drive, and a jam jar of Lisa's home-made kimchi.

Val eats another tangerine and half the box of almonds. Perhaps it was just low blood sugar. Across the aisle, Frank's Hot Sauce has finally shut up and pulled out a laptop. He shares a pair of headphones with his seatmate. Val takes an almond out of the box and takes aim to peg each boy in the side of the head. Just as she is about to launch the attack, Frank's Hot Sauce turns to look in her direction. She pops the almond into her mouth and starts to count.

The Megabus skids sharply to the right.

Her seatmate bolts upright. Frank's Hot Sauce and friend counter the skid by leaning left. Val grips the divider in front of her with both hands. The middle fingernail on her right hand is still painted a deep plum colour and the pinky on her left hand Pepsi-Cola blue. If this is how it was going to end, if she and a Megabus full of students were going to be strewn about the motorized leviathan before being flung into the ditch somewhere off the 401, at the very least she was going out with a semi-intact multi-coloured manicure.

The Megabus skids left.

Frank and friend lean right. There is shouting and crying at the back of the bus, and the pretty girl beside her grips the divider next to Val. No instructions were given at the time of boarding so Val instinctively reverts to airplane-emergency procedures. There is no oxygen mask on the Megabus so she leans forward and puts her head between her knees and exhales. A green aluminum water bottle rolls past her inverted head and down the steps to the lower level. On her next inhale, even though she is upside down, she visualizes her diaphragm lifting, expanding. *Lengthen, for fuck's sake. Elongate!*

The Megabus pivots around itself.

She keeps her head clamped firmly between her legs.

The swirling tilt-a-whirl sweeps around in a tsunami of emotion and she finally gets it, her very own, custom-designed pause button. *This* is what finding her centre is all about. It's the lack of any centre at all! She claims the space as her own, eyes closed, just as Clive had done on stage so many months ago. She is finally in a place where there is no room for fragility or achievement or perseverance, no agitation or restlessness or regret. The place is not out of reach anymore, because she is clutching it desperately, right here, right now. This colossal revolving axis is home to the focus she has been searching for, and it isn't difficult or complicated at all. In fact, it's pure and effortless and full of light.

NATURAL LIFE

"We should probably get started," *Tanis said. She flipped to a* fresh page in her notebook. "I have to know. How did you think you wouldn't get caught?"

Kellie stared at the dirty table between them. It was covered with smudges, pencil markings, a deep gouge, and a faded ring from a coffee cup.

"It was Craig's idea."

"That doesn't answer the question."

"He had it worked out."

"But what was he thinking?" Tanis asked. "What were you thinking?"

The prison authorities had agreed to give Tanis exactly one hour for the interview. They walked her to a room with a mirrored window and walls the colour of putty. Plain table with two metal chairs and fluorescent lighting that bathed the space in a disquieting hue. Kellie was already there when she arrived. Hands clasped loosely in front of her. No handcuffs or makeup. She wore an orange jumpsuit and had the same short haircut she'd had in grade seven, fourteen years ago, the last time they had seen each other. Her hair looked unwashed, and she wore a cheap pair of glasses. Her face was sallow, the same colour as the drab walls.

They had spent the first five minutes talking about how weird this was. What were the odds? How, after so many years, had they come together like this? Tanis kept the conversation on a surface level, the kind of small talk she loathed, because now that she was here, she felt that she couldn't rush the interview, even if she was under a time restriction. Just yesterday, she had reviewed her notes during the day-long journey from Regina to Phoenix, including the four-hour layover in Toronto where she momentarily contemplated not getting on the connecting flight. Even now that she was here, face to face with Kellie, she felt wavering and uncertain. She needed the interview to be stellar, a behind-the-scenes exclusive that would earn her the director's credit she coveted. She had even rehearsed her questions aloud this morning on the panicky drive to the prison in her rental car.

Kellie proceeded to tell her how they'd been given mouldy yogurt and stale bread for breakfast again. Tanis could have at least brought Kellie a banana or a dinky muffin from the continental buffet in the lobby of the Phoenix Airport Holiday Inn, though the guards would have probably taken the food away. But Tanis had slept through her alarm and neglected to order a wake-up call, and in her frantic rush out of the hotel hadn't stopped for anything to eat, not even coffee. She couldn't be late. She'd been in such a hurry she forgot her audio recorder, which was unlike her, an especially unprofessional move with the new job title on the line like this. She tried to put it out of her head and wiped her palms on her faux suede pants.

Kellie and Craig's story had slipped under the radar because they weren't as high profile as other Canadian criminals. But when Judy, the executive producer of the series, had found out that Tanis had a personal connection, she insisted on an initial interview.

"Go fishing," Judy had said. "See what you can catch."

"It was, like, years ago. We were kids."

"Then you'll have plenty to talk about."

"What do you think she's going to tell me?"

"I can't answer that. That's why you need to go."

She would rather do any other story. Maybe Judy would change her mind.

"Tanis. Opportunities like this are rare. Prove yourself for real this time."

Tanis was still on thin ice with Judy after she'd gone behind her back on another show they had worked on. Tanis had been a production assistant on a series of profiles of Canadian celebrities, not even a field producer as she was now. The musician Steven Page had been given his own episode, and Tanis wanted to do the interview so badly that she had pleaded directly with the show's director for weeks. When they were finally on set, the director let her do the interview under his supervision. He was a veteran who told her that he admired her drive and determination. In the end, she'd done a decent job, but Judy was pissed and warned her to watch her step.

The buzz in the room from the overhead light was like a drill to Tanis's skull. She should have worn a different shirt, not this stupid sweater. It was March in Arizona and the room had no vent. The only caffeine she'd had was a few sips from the bottle of flat Diet Coke she'd left in the rental car overnight. Pressure was building in her right temple.

"I just did what he said," Kellie said. Her words gurgled with phlegm and she coughed, unable to clear what was there.

"And it didn't occur to you to try and stop him?"

"Everything is bigger here, don't you think? Like the mountains."

"Sorry, what's that got to do with it?"

"It feels easier to hide because everything around you is extra large."

"Are you saying you and Craig were trying to hide here?"

Tanis wrote down the incongruous thought—hiding, large mountains—the details might be helpful in the report she needed to submit.

"He thought we could have a better life here."

"So you didn't try to persuade him to not do it? Didn't tell him it was a very bad idea?"

"He probably would have killed me too."

Tanis had had a fitful sleep and the fibres of her wool sweater were pricking her skin like a hundred pins, but she sat perfectly still, as if in a meditation pose.

"So he threatened you."

"What do you think?"

"It doesn't matter what I think."

"Craig was a very determined guy." Kellie nodded, like she had rehearsed the line.

"What will you tell your son?"

"You don't have kids, do you?" Kellie said, the slightest hint of a smile.

Tanis shook her head.

"The truth, I guess," Kellie said.

Tanis didn't speak—a trick she had learned as an intern, watching experienced directors conduct interviews. She tried to ignore her throbbing head and her irritated skin by focusing on the nick in the surface of the table that separated them.

"I'll answer his questions like I'm doing with you now," Kellie said.

There was a steadiness in Kellie's tone. Assured. Like when they were kids and living on the same street back in Weyburn, Saskatchewan. They had shared childhood secrets. Tanis wondered if Kellie even remembered them. The summer when they were nine years old, they played Barbies, and an innocent game of make-believe took a strange turn that they never spoke about afterward. They were in Tanis's backyard having a pool party with the dolls, using a green basin for a pool and washcloths as beach towels.

Kellie took her doll's bikini top off and said, "This is what they do in Europe."

Then she lifted up her own tank top, exposing her flat chest, and giggled.

"You should take your halter top off," Kellie said.

Tanis felt a strange tingling sensation in her shorts, knowing that what they were doing was wrong and that they could get caught at any second. There hadn't been any traffic in the alley behind the house for over half an hour and the cedar shrubs prevented anyone from seeing into the yard. When Tanis undid the tie at the back of her neck, some clouds passed overhead and blocked the sun. The shade gave her a sudden chill.

"I'm just kidding," Kellie said, pulling her top back down, but leaving the Barbie's bikini off. "Dean makes me do that sometimes."

Dean was Kellie's older brother, who had a reputation for being a bully and a pervert. Tanis knew that Dean's demands weren't right, but she didn't know what to say about it and so she had said nothing.

"You have freezies, right?" Kellie asked.

"Yeah, of course, yeah," Tanis said, flushed, retying the bow at the back of her neck. She was ready for twenty freezies.

It had been fourteen years since Tanis and Kellie had had any contact. They were twelve years old when Kellie's dad got transferred from Weyburn to Calgary for his job with the CN. Now this. Now, she was sitting across a grubby table in a Maricopa County prison, questioning her childhood friend about her involvement in a first-degree murder. What *were* the odds?

Kellie was craving salt and vinegar chips. It was like Tanis's presence brought up some memory of what they used to eat back in Weyburn. Last night's menu was watered-down orange juice and stale corn on the cob. Tanis Meyer. She had porked out since they had last seen each other. Stress probably. Maybe she binge ate because her fancy job in TV stressed her out. The lights in the interrogation room or whatever it was called were a lot brighter than in her bunk. The notice about the interview request came in the mail drop she'd been shown at orientation. It was the only mail she'd received in the six months she'd been there. Some of the other women had family members send them chocolate bars—candy bars, like the Americans said—Bounty and Three Musketeers. Not a Kit Kat to be found. Her boots were too tight, so she reached down under the table and undid the laces another inch. She had them tied extra tight for her walk on the outside track, which she'd done earlier this morning. The blue sky on the other side of the mountains was like something out of a movie. Too perfect of a colour. Looked made up. Kellie walked while the guards kept watch, always watching from their hardwood chairs. Always under surveillance. Even now in the interview. She wasn't sure if her hearing was going for real or if she was imagining it, but a ringing had started at some point, she couldn't say when exactly, because the days ticked forward like the second hand on an old clock. The noise was a constant high-pitched squeal that never went away, like those bugs in the summer that sound like a saw that won't shut off. The ringing started to be comforting after a while, something she could call her own; even if she had no control over it, even if was annoying, it was hers and she owned it. And in jail, where Kellie was just a number, one among many, she was more alone than she had ever been. She had signed the release form before Tanis arrived. Signed away the rights to her own story. But if anyone were to ask, she would say yes, it was nice to have a visitor for a change.

Tanis put her pen on the table. She took the hair elastic from her wrist and pulled her curly brown hair into a ponytail.

"What did it feel like?" Tanis asked.

Kellie nodded again. She smiled. Her face was that of a child, looking for forgiveness, recognition.

"You should talk to Craig."

That is what Tanis had told Judy. Craig was the story here, not Kellie. When the murder happened, it had been front-page news in Weyburn, a complete shock to the community. *How in the world, I don't believe it*, etc. For the series, Tanis had wanted to read Philip Zimbardo's book, *The Lucifer Effect: Understanding How Good People Turn Evil*, but she ran out of time and ended up watching his TED Talk, *The Psychology of Evil*, instead. She started to research psychopathic behaviour and read online articles by notable psychiatrists. She read essays by crime writers and noted bits of information that were relevant to her report.

She had come across a newspaper article about Russell Williams and the science behind a psychopathic mentality. It read: "All the while, he wore the mask of sanity ... That's also the measure of a cunning psychopath: He's often the last guy you'd ever suspect."

Tanis had told Judy that Kellie was the smaller story behind the real story. She was just an accomplice.

"Exactly," Judy said. "It's more interesting."

"You really want to know *her* side of things?" Tanis said.

"You're not thinking like a director."

"Kellie didn't plan the thing, she just went along with it."

"How do you know that?"

She was right, Tanis didn't know for sure. It was just what all the papers had reported.

"She's like a pawn."

"Bingo!" Judy said. "She's Everyman. She's your childhood pal, for Christ's sake. Don't you want to know what happened? Don't you want to know what makes a person participate in that kind of evil?"

Tanis did and she didn't.

"Yeah, but *he*'s the one who got life."

"And her? What is it, twenty-five years? Semantics," Judy said. "You're going."

When they were in grade six, Tanis would sometimes go to Kellie's house after school where they would eat Viva Puffs and watch music videos on the downstairs TV, trying to imitate Britney Spears' dance moves. It was Kellie's brother, Dean, who was the rebel in the family. Once, Kellie and Tanis followed Dean and his friend Tyler outside without them knowing. They went down by the ravine behind their house and watched the boys catch frogs by cupping them in their bare hands, then pulled their legs off one at a time.

Being at Kellie's place was always weird and exciting compared to being around Tanis's family. Kellie's mom was a nervous woman who always looked ready to defend herself. Her dad was a red-faced, red-haired guy who was over the top in the nicey-nice way he talked to them. He was too smiley. Tanis thought it was to cover up the fact that he didn't like his job on the railway. If he came home from his shift and found them dancing in the basement, he'd always say the same thing with a clownish grin on his beet-coloured face.

"There's Frick and Frack, up to no good again!"

Once he came home and didn't realize that Tanis and Kellie were down there and slammed the front door. Kellie pulled Tanis into the cubbyhole under the stairs where they had to crouch in squatting positions to fit.

"I know that slam," she whispered.

Her dad barrelled down the steps in his work boots and started to throw tools around his workbench—hammers, sandpaper blocks, screwdrivers. The girls were silent as statues, holding their breath.

"He can't find his lucky charm for the casino," Kellie mouthed the words at Tanis. "He gets like this when Mom cleans up too much."

The clamor continued, and they heard him muttering, "Where the fuck?" and "Stupid bitch."

Then the footsteps got closer to the stairs where they were hiding and Tanis squeezed Kellie's arm as hard as she could, but Kellie didn't budge an inch. It was as if she was made of stone. Then her dad opened the door to the cold storage room, pushed some boxes off the shelf, and slammed that door shut too. He made a grunting sound like an angry pig and headed back upstairs.

"Is he drunk?" Tanis asked.

Kellie said, "Not this time." Then she chewed off a piece of her fingernail and spit it at the wall. "Just really superstitious."

Kellie moved to another finger and gnawed some more.

Tanis shifted her feet, which were starting to cramp up, and asked what the lucky charm was.

"A dream-catcher keychain," Kellie said.

Later, Kellie told Tanis about the time her dad caught her with a cigarette—a butt she'd stolen from Dean—and how he hit her with a wooden hanger on the back of her legs. Another time when he couldn't find the dream-catcher, he took the rolling pin to her back. The bruises were always in places people couldn't see, so she was able to keep it a secret.

Back in the interview, Tanis said, "I would love to talk to Craig, but he's an unwilling participant."

"He's very private," Kellie said.

"Tell me what it felt like."

"I didn't do much."

"You killed a person."

"I helped. I guess I did that."

Zimbardo's TED Talk listed the first of the social processes that greased the slippery slope of evil as "mindlessly taking the first small step."

In elementary school, they had gone on a field trip in the middle of winter. Miss Wintonick took it upon herself to educate her grade five class about winter survival techniques in the prairies. Miss Win, as everyone fondly called her, piled twenty-eight ten-year-olds onto a bus and drove twenty kilometres out of town. Tanis and Kellie and the others strapped on snowshoes and carried backpacks full of extra socks, matches, and instant noodles out into a barren field. Their steps were like hole punches in the snow; they were breaking ground like pioneers. The prairie wind made frostbite a concern for any exposed skin. Ice crystals formed on their scarves, and everyone had rivers of snot running from their noses. They finally stopped in a sheltered area, the only clump of trees for miles. Tasked with collecting kindling, Tanis and Kellie headed away from the group. Two hundred yards away from where the class was setting up camp, the girls came across an injured sparrow sitting on the snow at the base of a tree. Its wing was damaged, fluttering and shaking, its little brown eyes were two shiny beads of panic. Kellie picked up a twig and wedged it under the bird's chest, and the fluttering increased, a heightened sense of distress.

"We should take it back with us," Tanis said.

"For what?" Kellie said.

"Maybe Miss Win will want to keep it."

The snow was at least two feet deep below the crust. Kellie stood up and brought her latticed snowshoe down on the bird, crushing its entire existence into the white below.

The light in the interview room started to flicker. Kellie didn't flinch.

"It does that sometimes," she said. "Power shortages or whatever."

There was a loose piece of yarn on the sleeve of Tanis's sweater, and if she pulled it, the whole thing might unravel, which would be preferable at this point. She wasn't getting anywhere. The whole thing was itchy and uncomfortable. What was Judy going to say about her shitty field notes and no audio recording? Just her word. Nothing to transcribe.

Tanis could kill the story. She could tell Judy that Kellie was a dud who wouldn't talk. Her fishing trip had been a bust and the story wasn't worth pursuing. But Tanis could hear Judy's response. "Tough luck, kid, back to the research desk for you."

Forty minutes to go.

"So what does *helping* with a murder feel like?"

"Final," Kellie said. "Like an ending."

Tanis wrote this down. She had to write something down. The conversation was disjointed and sketchy, like a bad dream.

"The old lady's life, you mean?"

"That too," Kellie said. "Things are different now."

"I don't understand."

"It's stupid," Kellie said.

Kellie spoke in fragments and stared at the gouge in the table. She traced around it with each of her fingers, one by one.

"Try me."

"Part of my life ended out there in the desert," Kellie said.

Tanis noted this.

"It's such a repetition in here. They make you feel dead. I think that's what they want you to feel."

Kellie looked up and smiled thinly at Tanis. Misery, relief, resignation all in one. "And after a while, you start to think that that's how it should be."

The article about psychopathic behaviour also noted that in the part of the brain that involved emotions and self-control, deep in the paralimbic systems, the connections were weaker.

Then Kellie had a coughing fit. She said the water they were given tasted like chemicals, like chlorine. Tanis reached into her purse to offer Kellie a cough drop, then remembered the mirrored window and thought better of it.

Kellie could smell Tanis's shampoo from across the table, one of those fruity melon kinds. Kellie sat up straight and pressed her heels into the floor. She had been attracted to Craig from the minute he walked into the video store where she'd been working three years ago. He looked like a football player. He rented the new Batman or Spiderman movie and Kellie thought he seemed dangerous. Craig taught her to look people in the eye, and that's what she did with Tanis. It was hard but she did it. Inside her boots, she curled her toes under as far as she could because even a simple action like that helped her to focus, a habit she'd developed as a kid while her parents were yelling at each other or if Dean was trying to get her to break the windshield wipers off the neighbours' cars at night. She would curl her toes under or suck the skin on the inside of her cheek, which she did so hard sometimes she drew blood. Craig had the same kind of trick to calm himself down when he was getting heated. He made fists. He'd make fists and squeeze them as hard as he could until he couldn't take it any more. He held his hands at his sides until his knuckles turned white, and when he finally opened his hands his fingernails had pressed into the skin so hard they made little dotted lines in his palms.

Kellie wondered if Tanis remembered playing volleyball together back in Weyburn. They were both on the junior team and went to practices after school with coach Taylor, who always said that even if you were on the bench, you were in the game. Volleyball wasn't an aggressive sport. Not until you were playing it. Not until you really got to nail that ball. Kellie's forearms would be red and swollen at the beginning of the season from lack of practice, bruised and sore at first, but soon her skin got as leathery as the ball. She was a decent player, always up for an assist to make a point. Just like she had been Craig's assist. She'd nailed it. If there was anything Kellie had mastered in her first six months in prison, it was her ability to adapt. In jail, the issue of survival wasn't much different than when she was a kid. Back then, she survived by hiding under the stairs. Too bad she and Tanis couldn't go for a drink. Too bad they couldn't go have a nice cocktail in the hotel bar or drive to Phoenix and have a pancake lunch at IHOP.

The production company had received development funding for an investigative, *Fifth Estate* kind of documentary series with a focus on criminals who were sentenced to life. The working title was *Natural Life*—six one-hour shows. Along with stylized re-enactments, each episode was to include interviews with specialists and key characters: brain researchers, geneticists, psychiatrists, psychologists, prison wardens, family members, and the convicts themselves, where possible. On the whiteboard back in the Regina production office, Craig Bodnar's name was at the bottom of a list that included more recognized Canadian felons like Paul Bernardo, Robert Pickton, Russell Williams.

The show would rely on Tanis's personal relationship to reveal Kellie's psychological motivations as one half of the

Canadian couple who had brutally killed an Arizona woman, then attempted to steal her motor home. Judy had asked her to dig deep without making it sensational. *Prove yourself for real.* But this was asking for so much more than she'd had to do before. Steven Page hadn't gone out and murdered an innocent old woman. No matter how she came at it, no matter how long she thought about it, because she knew Kellie, the story left Tanis confused and angry.

Tanis first heard it on the news like everyone else, and as the saga unfolded, she began to poke around. She had learned that Kellie, Craig, and their infant son, Theo, had briefly lived in Apache Junction. They had used the town as their temporary home, where they staked out an elderly woman who was selling her motor home in a nearby town, Surprise. Apache Junction sat in the bottom of a valley in southern Arizona surrounded by the Superstitious Mountains. Weaver's Needle was a prominent landmark and rock-climbing destination, a jagged piece of rock that separated itself from the rest of the mountain range and could be seen from miles away.

"Why here?" Tanis said.

"Why not?"

Kellie was getting snarky, almost pushy. Like how she used to play volleyball. Quiet on the bench, aggressive in the game.

"We don't have to do this, you know."

Kellie looked Tanis in the eye, sucked in one of her cheeks, and said, "I don't know why. Craig liked the desert, I guess."

"We can stop any time."

"No."

Kellie sat up straighter in her chair. She pushed her shoulders back.

"Are you sure?"

"I want to do this." Kellie's voice was firm, in control, and Tanis remembered the Barbies. Kellie had called the shots back then and Tanis followed along.

Half an hour left. She pulled up the sleeves of her uncomfortable sweater. Move from the known to the unknown—that was how she had been taught to dissect a story. Ask too many questions, include the facts, but don't judge. A television hour is abridged, edited, heightened. The story needed to be balanced, unbiased, like a trial.

"I just don't get it," Tanis said. "I mean, Jesus, what makes a person do something like that?"

"I made a bad choice. We got caught. Simple."

Fuck. She wanted to get this damn sweater off. Get back on the plane and get the hell out of here. Get this over with.

"Where did you guys meet?"

"He came in to the video store I was working at."

"In Calgary?"

"Yeah. He was a big guy, he took charge," Kellie said. "I liked it."

Tanis wrote this down on her notepad.

"So it was good between you at first?"

"Yeah, sure." Kellie laughed out loud, a chuckle that morphed into a cough.

"And now?"

"Now?" Kellie poked at the scar in the tabletop. Her

fingernails were short and dirty. "Now I'm paying the price. We both are."

Then she chewed off a piece of her nail and spit it at the wall.

Another part of her research popped into Tanis's mind: Brains of psychopaths can be stunted. In some adults, the amygdalae, almond-shaped structures that are involved in the processing of memory and emotional reactions like fear and aggression, can be significantly smaller than normal.

Kellie described their life in Calgary where they had lived for two years. Craig had been fired from three construction jobs because, his employers told him, he made too many mistakes and was late all the time. Then she took a deep breath in through her nose, held it for several seconds, and released the air in one controlled exhale.

"We needed to make some changes," she said.

Kellie described the day they left Calgary. Craig had stolen the truck from the site where he'd been working, a half-built seniors' residence. She had the baby all ready to go when he picked them up. On their way out of the city, they passed a billboard with an ad for the seniors' centre, showing wide sidewalks and enticing sun porches.

"Sit there and wait to die," Craig had said. "We're going to do a lot better than that."

Tanis had read an interview on Showtime's website between Michael C. Hall, the actor who played the serial killer on *Dexter*, and Kevin Dutton, author of *The Wisdom of Psychopaths*. The author told the actor how there were two things that made psychopaths happy: instant gratification and control. Tanis couldn't believe that a person just wakes up one day with no moral responsibility or social conscience. Kellie was no psychopath. A few misguided decisions does not a murderer make. If that were the case, couldn't their roles have just as easily been reversed? If Tanis had hooked up with the wrong guy, would she be the one in an orange jumpsuit eating mouldy yogurt for breakfast? Tanis's family was pleasant and bland, the opposite of Kellie's. Tanis had been taught to suppress emotions and exercise complacency. The answers Tanis needed—*Why did you? How could you?*—may as well have been buried deep within the gouge in the table between them. She was as close to getting those answers out of Kellie as she was to climbing Weaver's Needle out in the Superstitious Mountains.

She bought the idea that everyone had the capacity to be kind or cruel; people were capable of extraordinary things in particular situations—like lifting cars off injured children. And under certain influences, people could do unthinkable things, like marrying a psychopath, for instance.

"How did he threaten you, exactly?"

Kellie sucked in her cheek and stared at the missing chunk in the table. She didn't say anything for almost a minute.

"He said he would have killed me too."

Tanis put down her pen. She ran her fingers up through the front part of her hair and massaged her temples.

"And I wonder if that would have been a better thing," Kellie said.

"Fuck." Tanis was holding back tears. "Of course not."

"Think about it."

"You obviously didn't want to die."

"Then, yeah. But now?" Kellie shrugged, coughed, shuffled her feet under the table.

"I just feel so sorry for you," Tanis said.

"Don't," Kellie said. "Don't feel that." Kellie shook her head and looked straight at Tanis. "Plus, I thought it didn't matter what you thought?"

Kellie pulled each of the pant legs of her jumpsuit forward at her thighs. The uniform was like canvas. Tanis's notepad reminded Kellie of when they were kids and used to make folded fortunes out of paper. It was a game. The fortunes said things like: *You'll have a happy life* or *You'll be rich*. But the girls always added details like how big their houses would be and where they would live— Paris, Los Angeles, Vancouver. The day Kellie found out her family had to move to Calgary, she got *You'll go on a trip* three times in a row before they even knew about the transfer. That day after school, Tanis and Kellie stopped at the drugstore on their way home to buy chips. They loitered in the store, flipping through fashion magazines and trying on perfume. On display near the cash, nestled in a box of black foam, was a selection of rhinestone rings. A handwritten sign in swirly cursive read: *Toe Rings $2.99*.

"Which one do you like?" Kellie asked, pulling out a ring that had two red gems bookending a white rhinestone.

Tanis pointed at one that had three clear light-blue stones in a row.

"My birthstone," she said.

Old Mrs Friesen who worked the cash was busy with another customer so Kellie slipped the two rings up into the cuff of her sweatshirt. Tanis held up a loonie and the bag of chips so Mrs Friesen could see them both, then left the coin on the counter. Everyone knew everyone in Weyburn. The old woman waved and nodded in her direction and the girls left the store.

On the sidewalk, Tanis asked, "You're not afraid of getting caught?"

Kellie shrugged and said, "It worked, didn't it?"

Then Kellie opened the bag of salt and vinegar chips while they walked to end of the block. They turned right onto Main Street at Yee's Chinese Food Restaurant and stopped to sit on the bench in front of City Hall.

"You didn't notice that I took this too," Kellie said, pulling out a silver tube of lipstick from her other shirtsleeve.

"Oh my God," Tanis said, taking the lipstick and reading the label on the bottom: "Jaunty plum."

Kellie handed Tanis the ring with the sparkly blue stones and said, "Something to remember me by."

But they lost touch after the move.

Kellie sensed that her calm, collected mask wasn't fooling Tanis during the interview. She sat up straight again. Pushed her heels into the floor. She had made a choice with Craig that, in the end, had given her no choice.

There was a kind of serenity that went along with being locked up, caged. She was boxed up like an animal, and there was comfort in that. Like the ringing in her ear. She might let her hair grow out. Get fat. Learn Spanish. She felt relieved, in a way. To feel the passing of time in slow motion like this. Her cough wouldn't go away. She got chills at night and didn't sleep; she had only a thin blanket and the mattress was bumpy and uneven. That nick in the table between them could hold an entire valley, a whole world waiting to crawl out and dance around the room. Kellie told Tanis how she and Craig had had some good times, like always ordering strawberry and banana French Toast at IHOP. It sure would be nice to have some bottled water, she thought, but that was asking too much and she knew it.

Fifteen minutes left.

"I'm just the field producer, you know," Tanis said. "The director has the final say of what goes on air."

"Okay," Kellie said.

Another section from the newspaper article tugged at Tanis: "Psychopaths tend to stay focused on a task. They can't—or don't—stop, despite signals and warnings from their environment, from morals, conscience, law, things other people would find hard to ignore."

"But they'll want to know the facts," Tanis said. "Your side of the story. Why you went along with it."

"Don't you have a recorder or something?" Kellie said.

"I forgot it at the hotel."

Kellie took pauses when she spoke so Tanis could get it all down. She explained how Craig had found the ad online for the old lady's motor home in the *Surprise Today*'s classifieds.

"Surprise," Kellie said. "I thought it was a funny name for a town."

"Sounds made up," Tanis said, laughing a little.

"That's what I thought."

And for the briefest moment it was as if they were two childhood friends who had accidentally run into each other and were catching up, having a laugh about an oddly named city.

"So Craig called the number and the old lady said that her family was moving her to an old folks' home. She called it a retirement residence."

Kellie told Tanis how Craig lied to the lady about how they were moving to the US for work. He said he had a job as a welder and they were going to rent a place in Apache Junction, but it was temporary.

One of the criteria listed by the American Psychiatric Association as part of Antisocial Personality Disorder, or psychopathy, was deceitfulness, as indicated by repeated lying, use of aliases, or conning others for personal profit or pleasure.

"So the murder was planned all along?" Tanis said.

Kellie nodded.

"Fuck." Tanis rubbed her forehead, pen in hand. "I just don't see how you could possibly think you wouldn't get caught."

"Craig did a lot of things and didn't get caught."

Tanis felt nauseous.

"There were others?"

"No, I mean stuff like stealing credit cards, ID, cars. It was easy for him."

"Stealing is a long way from murder, don't you think?"

"It starts somewhere," Kellie said. "He stole tons of stuff as a kid. After a while it started being normal."

"Normal."

"I don't expect you to understand."

Tanis needed to understand. It was her job to make other people understand. She had a flashback to Weyburn of Kellie shoplifting some jewellery, toe rings, one for each of them. A sign of their friendship a long time ago. Tanis might even still have the thing somewhere. She needed to be professional about this. But how was she going to break the story down so an audience could form their own opinions about what happened if she couldn't grasp it herself?

"Go on. When you got to the trailer. Tell me about that."

Kellie recounted the event step by step as if it were a recipe. She had a roll of duct tape tucked under the baby blanket in the diaper bag. She did everything Craig said. Nodded to the lady when they arrived at the motor home. Looked around like they were interested buyers.

"It smelled old in there," Kellie said. "There were lumpy crocheted doilies on the table, like at my grandma's, and a spoon collection. A souvenir Statue of Liberty by the sink. There were a lot of books. Some of them blocked the light from the small windows. When the old lady turned around to show us the bedroom at the back, Craig pushed her and she fell."

"And what were you thinking then?" Tanis said, leaning forward. "In that moment."

"That she didn't matter anymore."

Like that bird, the little sparrow, back in grade five.

"The old lady?"

"Yeah."

"Is that what he told you to think?"

Zimbardo's second social process that greased the slippery slope of evil was "the dehumanization of others."

Tanis wasn't convinced. Putting a half-dead bird out of its misery when you were ten years old was different from assisting with first-degree murder.

Kellie's gaze was fixed on the chip in the table. She covered it with her palm.

"Well," she said, as the childish smile returned to her face. "She *was* pretty old. Why shouldn't *we* have a chance?"

"At the expense of someone else's life?"

Kellie took her hand off the table and lowered her head as if she was going to pray. She told the rest of the story like that. She said that, as planned, she had given Craig the tape after he knocked the woman down, and she took the baby outside while he finished. The baby was fidgety on her hip when she walked back to the road and waited. She looked up at Tanis momentarily.

"Theo put his hands up to his ears," she said and put her own hands up to her ears. "That's what he did when he was tired."

What story were they going to put on TV? The ability to perpetrate evil is ever-present. There is a diabolical part of human nature lying dormant in all of us, and all it takes is a certain set of circumstances to allow it to come pouring out. If this could happen to someone like Kellie, couldn't it happen to anyone?

Tanis was overthinking this. She remembered reading

something online that referenced an "overfocusing" hypothesis. It suggested that psychopaths devote so much attention to things of immediate interest that they effectively ignore other input.

The nausea hadn't stopped. Her armpits were damp. The interview was almost over, and she had to make this work. She would suggest a treatment for the story, would write the whole damn script for the show to make up for her carelessness on this trip. She would recommend that she come back with a camera crew to do the location shoot. Reveal the beauty of the desert through slow, expansive pans of the Superstitious Mountains. Highlight the desolation of the area as a metaphor to illustrate Kellie's isolation. Show close-ups of cactus plants, snakes, and lizards. Drop clues about what leads a person down the path to evil. Let Kellie talk, but leave the viewer to form their own opinion. Make the story unbiased and fair, make it seem that, yes, it could happen to anyone. Distort the brutality in post-production with jump cuts and high contrast, oversaturated images. She jotted her ideas down quickly in point form.

Ten minutes to go.

Kellie asked Tanis to tear a sheet of paper from her notepad. She folded the corner over once and then the other way, making a triangle, then ran her finger along the edge where there was an extra inch and tore that bit off. She folded the square into the middle, turned it over, and did it again. She kept folding and turning it, but it in the end it was too small. She could hardly get her fingers inside from the bottom to do the back and forth motion.

"Remember this?" Kellie said. "You'll go on a trip." She handed the paper to Tanis.

Craig had told Kellie that among animals in the wild, the strong outrun the weak. On the prairies, coyotes pick out sick and injured prey—gophers, hedgehogs, muskrat—and allow the strong and healthy ones to survive.

Prior to the trip, Tanis read an article in the *Calgary Herald* that cited Craig as having "some evidence of organic brain damage in his youth."

"Did *you* think the old lady deserved to die?"

Kellie shook her head. It was hardly noticeable.

"It wasn't like the bird, was it?" Tanis said.

"What bird?"

"Winter survival with Miss Win. Grade five."

"I don't remember."

"You killed that sparrow we found with the broken wing."

Tanis leaned back. On her notepad, she was sketching the sharp point of Weaver's Needle. A lonesome peak in a sea of rock.

"That's why Craig wanted to come here," Kellie said, nodding at the sketch. "The exotic landscape."

"Pretty far from home," Tanis said.

"He wanted a new start."

Tanis made another note to herself: "More *Lucifer*. Expanding on the fictional notion about the power of anonymity to unleash violent behaviour. Like William Golding's *Lord of the Flies*."

"Tell me again how you thought you wouldn't get caught," Tanis said.

"Get rid of the evidence," Kellie answered softly. Then she tried to clear her throat, but it sounded like more of a growl.

Tanis had read that psychopaths were as rational as anyone, probably even more than most people, because their thoughts weren't cluttered by the noise of human emotions.

Kellie explained that after Craig had beaten, bound, and gagged the woman, he ran over her with her own motor home. He set the body on fire and they drove north in the stolen vehicle. Tanis reached down and fished through her bag for another pen. There wasn't one. She found a stubby pencil she hadn't known was there. When Tanis sat back up, Kellie looked her straight in the eye and said, "No. It wasn't like the bird at all."

Kellie's lower lip started to quiver. She blinked hard. Her shoulders slumped forward. She brought her hands back up onto the tabletop, fingers clasped so tight that they weren't skin-coloured anymore, just a stacked jumble of red and white digits.

"We're different, you and me," Kellie said.

"That still doesn't answer the question."

"What question?"

"How could you go along with it?"

"I told you. Choice," Kellie said without hesitation. "You can talk yourself into believing anything is a good choice if you try hard enough."

"Can you?" Tanis said.

Kellie coughed again. Used the back of her hand to wipe her nose.

"Remember my dad? I used to talk myself into thinking that whenever he hit me, or my mom, it was for our own good. After a while it just started to feel normal."

Zimbardo's seventh and final step was "passive tolerance of evil through inaction or indifference."

They had only a few minutes left. Tanis wasn't taking notes anymore. She was doodling while Kellie spoke, sketching boxes and squares. Drawing spiky cactus plants and sharp-edged mountains.

"I wish it didn't turn out this way," Tanis said.

"Yeah, but it did."

Kellie pawed at the nick in the table then tapped at it like the table was red-hot.

"What will happen to Theo?" Tanis said.

"He's with Craig's parents."

"What's going to happen when Theo finds out, when he learns the truth?"

"I don't know," Kellie said. Her voice was hard and convincing. "No one knows that."

With the little pencil, Tanis traced the letter *y* in the word *baby*, over and over on her notepad. The repetition made the paper weak and lead marked the page beneath.

Kellie didn't get any other visitors. Her parents had cut off all communication, and she had stopped talking to Dean after he left home. Now she had told Tanis the whole story in her own words. Sitting there across from her, Tanis appeared calmer than at the beginning of the interview. Maybe the truth was starting to sink in. There was nothing she could do about what happened and she would never ever understand it, even if they did put it on TV. It wouldn't change anything. Earlier, Tanis had been agitated; she had a lot of questions and wanted to get it all right.

When Kellie was first sent to jail, she was sick all the time. Just thinking about those early days made her dizzy. Now it was just the cough. Just another thing to accept. Nothing bad had ever happened to Tanis, Kellie thought, so she didn't know about desperation and bad choices. Maybe that's why she got a job on a TV show, so she could try to sort out other people's stories, because she didn't have one of her own. Tanis's parents were teachers, not shift workers. Tanis's family spent summer vacations at their cabin at Kenosee Lake or visiting relatives in British Columbia.

Had Kellie been convincing enough? Would she even get to be on TV? Would Tanis come back and visit if it wasn't for research? On her notepad, Tanis had drawn two squares connected by four lines that made a cube and gave the illusion of being 3D. It was a simple trick. All you had to know was where to connect the points.

When Tanis asked if there was anything else Kellie wanted her to include in the report, Kellie told her how Craig took her fishing for pike one spring to Sylvan Lake. They took the bus out to Airdrie and stayed with his Uncle Walt. Walt drove them to the lake, where they stayed out on the water until dusk, hauling in more than the legal limit. Afterwards, the men gutted the pike, and they went back to Walt's where they had a huge fish fry and got wasted.

"Craig always said the best way to kill a fish was to knock it hard against the head after you'd hooked it. Put it out of its misery. I don't remember your dad telling us to do it that way, do you?" Kellie said.

The summer Tanis and Kellie were seven years old, Kellie had gone on vacation with Tanis's family to Kenosee Lake. Tanis's dad let them fish off the dock. Each of them caught a six-inch pike that afternoon, and Tanis's mom had taken a photo. Both girls sported proud toothy grins and held up their catches, which Tanis's dad had hung from a stick, green and silver scales gleaming in the sun.

Tanis's report, in part, read:

Kellie (Feschuk) Bodnar had wanted what everyone wants: security, purpose, happiness. She married a man because his offer of a good life was too good to pass up. He provided for her. Kellie is delusional and a dreamer and too immature to be a good mother. No marketable skills, no post-secondary education. Trauma, neglect and/or early childhood abuse may be influential in her behaviour (psychiatrist to analyze/expand re: does she have actual psychopathic tendencies). She is a person who made an extraordinarily bad choice. A person who convinced herself this is the life she deserves.

Possible additional interviews (TBC): state police, psychiatrist, residents of the Lost Dutchman RV Park, prison warden. Potentials: Craig (unlikely), the victim's family, Craig's parents. (Note: at the time of writing, Craig's parents have applied for official custody of Theo, Craig and Kellie's eighteen-month-old son.)

A good writer could twist the plot and make it seem like she was better off in jail. The series could show how, behind bars, Kellie had become enlightened. Tucked away in a prison cell, she had found a place to belong. Within a range of dusty orange mountains, she was Weaver's Needle personified: a woman alone, separated from the rest of society.

Tanis had one last question that Kellie repeated back to her.

"If I could go back, would I change things?"

Kellie covered a cough with her hand. Made a fist. Left it balled up in front of her lips. She shivered then and it looked like she was shaking off a chill from a fever.

Tanis looked at the squares on her notepad, squares and lines, an attempt to organize things that she couldn't understand into manageable units. Simplify the complicated.

Kellie rubbed at a spot on the table as if to polish it clean or get rid of it, Tanis couldn't tell. "I would do anything if I could change this," Kellie said.

Tanis left herself enough time to tour the area in the rental car before she had to be at the airport. She took photos with a digital camera. An exterior of the prison, the fence surrounding the structure, an outhouse in the RV park, the city limits sign for Surprise, a close-up of a cactus, and Weaver's Needle backlit by a tangerine sky, a stunning image.

She followed the path they took. Grey and lofty, dirty clouds hung above the road they'd left behind, where dry flames licked the horizon. Where Kellie held her baby, who fidgeted and cried while bands of oily smoke crawled into the sky like a nest of snakes in search of prey. Tanis drove away with the windows open, and the air smelled of diesel.

In the rear-view mirror, the road shrank away behind her. She kept driving and reached up, tilting the mirror so she couldn't see.

THE ROGUES AND SCOUNDRELS AMONG US

Dear Company T—,

I need you to know it disappoints me to have to write this. In a negative situation, I try my best to see the positive side, but you have not made this easy. We all face challenges in life and work, but I am the kind of person who takes pride in what I do. Among other things, I wash the floors and vacuum the hall carpets at Bridgeside Manor. I sort out the junk mail for the tenants and organize the garbage and recycling for pickup. Tenants have told me, "You did a very nice job with the flowers out front." Or, "You keep that recycling room in such good order, Yvonne, thank you." It's a good job that keeps me grounded so I am able to cope with more difficult situations in life. Situations like what happened with Joan. Situations like you.

First, I must tell you that I will not be recommending your product to anyone in the building. You should know the apartment block has seven floors with forty units per floor, with plenty of women living in those units—including a few womanly men—who might have used your alleged eco-friendly hair-removal kit from time to time, but now they'll never know about it unless they randomly find it on the drugstore shelf, like I did. It is worth mentioning I have some influence on these people, their lifestyle choices and shopping habits.

Second, I am enclosing a self-addressed stamped envelope so you can send my money back. I realize it's only twelve dollars (plus the thirteen percent harmonized sales tax we pay in Ontario), but given the circumstances, I feel that this is fair. Did your customer service rep, Fatima, tell you I nearly went to the emergency room? What I am looking for is closure and peace of mind after what has been a very trying experience. You, in the public service industry, can surely understand that. Your customer satisfaction guarantee is written right there on the box. It says: *If you're not satisfied, just return any new or unused product to us within thirty (30) days from the date of purchase, and we'll refund the full purchase price.*

I am also writing to ask you, Company T—, for a fifty-dollar credit to the chain store Winners. I feel that, in addition to the refund, further compensation is necessary. I do a lot of my shopping at Winners because of their quality and service. My old friend Joan introduced me to the place years ago because she was a stylish dresser but refused to pay full retail. It should be simple enough for you to go on the Internet and purchase the gift card to include in the previously mentioned self-addressed stamped envelope. The fifty dollars will cover the cost of a pair of pants that, because of the incident, I was forced to purchase. Their head office is just outside Toronto, Ontario, the city where I live and work. I know this because I have written them letters of thanks. Thank you letters are the kinds of letters

I am accustomed to writing, not something like this. I would be happy to send you one should I receive the fifty-dollar gift card, but that remains to be seen.

Please note I have included receipts for twelve tablets of Benadryl ($5.26, tax included) and two aloe plants ($8.00 each—no tax because the Asian fellow who owns the plant store on the corner by my place doesn't charge it if I pay cash). I encourage you to use your judgment on what to do with these. There is a DVD rental that I ought to get reimbursed for as well, but I have more decency than that.

Third, a note about the information printed on the piece of paper included with the kit regarding your return policy. Please explain why the print needs to be so small. I had to get out my magnifying glass to read it because I am quite sure you didn't want me, or any other honest, hard-working consumer, to actually know what it said. It's not only your company who makes this print difficult to read. That, I'll give you. It's everyone, selling anything—cars, pepper grinders, those running shoes with an inch of foam on the bottom that claim to work by just standing there, even laundry detergent. That fine print, as you know, says: *You are entitled to a refund of your purchase if: a) The item was defective or damaged b) It was not what you ordered or c) You are unsatisfied with the results of the product.*

I am not even sorry about not recommending your defective little kit. In fact, I might even go out of my way to tell people *not* to use it and that is very out of character for me. I might even ask my boss, Drakkar, if I can put a note up in the recycling room in the locked glass cabinet by the door. I have put things in there like notices for furniture for sale or parking spaces for rent, and I think a warning about your product wouldn't hurt.

Fourth, a word about your customer service representatives. When I called the help line, I spoke to a woman with an exotic accent, maybe Saudi Arabian, who treated me like I was her best friend in the whole world. I am fifty-eight years old and, by choice, don't have many friends. It's not like I am some kind of hermit. Like I said, everyone in the building knows me. And even amidst the trauma of my failed attempt with your "simple to use" organic kit, I managed to make it to Montreal to see my old friend Joan. We had had a falling out and if our friendship was to ever stand a chance, this trip was an important step in rebuilding it.

Have you ever had to ride the subway after sandpapering your legs? Try it sometime. It might help you empathize with your customers. Joan had said it was even hotter in Montreal, which sounded a little far-fetched, but I left it alone. I packed only what I would need for the two nights at her place and had my suitcase tucked behind my irritated legs under the subway seat because it was small enough to be a carry-on. Because of all the aloe gel, I knew I would have to check it when I got to the airport. I had learned this from my e-ticket (more fine print) because Drakkar was nice enough to print it out for me at work since I don't have a printer at home. That's Drakkar for you, generous and thoughtful and helping people out. Didn't even give it a second thought. The e-ticket provided a list of items you can't have in your carry-on that included liquids and aerosols and lighters and axes. Axes! Who takes an axe on a plane?

It was only twenty-five minutes to Union station, but the subway was so warm that the stinging on my legs was getting worse by the second. I was using the station stops to regulate my breathing so when the voice of the subway said, "Arriving at Osgoode. Osgoode station," I let all the air out of my mouth slow and steady like my relaxation CD said to do. I was concerned because Joan said there might be a pool party while I was there. She said there was a rooftop pool in her building. The thought of exposing my heinously scraped and tender shins in public was enough to give me the chills.

So when that ethnic lady on the other end of your 1-800 product help line started calling me *dear* and *darling*, it was off-putting. Her honey-coated voice was so nice I couldn't help being suspicious. I've been burned by that kind of sweet talk before. I'm not going to get into how I found that out the hard way years ago, by marrying someone from Cuba who I thought was the real thing. The rogues and scoundrels among us manipulate situations to suit their selfish needs and I can't help but see the parallel with your product. Those wax strips are not quick, not easy, and certainly not mess-free. The similarity to my marriage is uncanny. But like I said, I try to see the positive side of things. I'm trying right now. And I hope, Company T—, you will not let me down.

Do you think it's easy to write a letter like this? Do you think I enjoy it? Experiences like this harden a person. But after listening to your customer service rep's advice I almost thought I might try the product again at some point. Maybe she was right and I was doing it wrong. When I told her how I had put the strips on and all the hair didn't come off in one yank and I proceeded to go over the same patch of skin again and again, she sucked in her breath. She said she sympathized with me and told me it was a first-timer's poor luck. In an even smoother, polished silver way she said, "Perhaps you need to relax next time. The process is not something to be rushed." That charming softy almost had me until I looked down and saw my two splotchy, skinless chicken legs.

It's a wonder I didn't need skin grafts.

I have revealed too much already which is why I am not even going to mention the situation that developed when, with just the one strip, I tried to do my bikini line.

I'm not going to lie, my friendship with Joan did not end well. In a way, that customer service rep of yours reminded me of her. That self-important, uppity way Joan used to speak to me. No matter what I had going on, Joan had something worse. When I told her about getting the job at Bridgeside Manor and how Drakkar was a good boss, I didn't even say handsome, all she said was, "Oh yeah," and went on to tell me how her office was getting new furniture.

When I told Joan about adopting Bernadette, the little dog that was orphaned because her owner, Brenda, who lived in Bridgeside Manor (#414), died in a plane crash, all she did was tell me a story about an emergency landing she had on a flight to Chicago once. Not a word about my new situation with Bernadette.

Maybe this was how it was all meant to happen. The waxing, my break-up with Joan, Bernadette. Not everyone is comfortable with dogs. Joan sure wasn't. Bernadette is about half the size of a normal clock radio, and her wiry white fur is almost all gone except for a tuft on the top of her head and some on her legs. Her pink skin shows through all over her body and she's got tear stains next to her bugged-out eyes. She looks like a dwarf piglet. The vet said I could try melatonin for the hair loss and told me to break up a pill into granular bits and add it to her food. The bottle he showed me listed cautions and warnings and possible side effects. (Covered in fine print.) I told him I didn't think giving melatonin to Bernadette was a good idea at all. Her brain is as big as a grape, but she can't be fooled that easily. She'd have caught on to the drugs in her food for sure.

At night when I'm lying in bed staring at the ceiling, wondering if I will ever tell Drakkar how I feel, Bernadette nuzzles her little snout into my neck. One time she did that, and I thought it was a spider! When I tried flicking it away, I flung her clear off the bed onto the floor! I carried the poor little thing around like a baby for an hour before she finally stopped shaking. To make it up to her I bought her a box of cheese and bacon flavoured dog biscuits. I gave her two right off the bat and told her that it was not my intention to toss her off the bed like that. I think in her bottle-cap-sized heart she understood, and she has forgiven me. Because now she rolls on her side and exposes her sheer belly to me, looking for a tummy rub, and probably another one of those treats.

What happened with Joan was that I finally got fed up with her bossiness and self-centred attitude and stopped answering her calls. Eventually, she stopped calling altogether. The whole thing stressed me out so much, I took up meditation. Francesca, a woman who lives in #520 and has a taffy-coloured poodle, noticed the change in my behaviour and recommended a book called *The Mindful Way through Depression*. I didn't take it personally because I know she was just trying to help. The book came with a CD that guides you through a series of meditations. I also made up a private mantra that I still use when things get difficult.

Bridgeside Manor is like that, full of considerate people with manners, even the ones who rent. But I will say this: Things are not always what they seem. Like Joan, for example. Like your product. Maybe those strips are "simple to use" for some people, but not me. Maybe some people can just go out into the world and find someone who will love them for who they are, but for me, it hasn't happened yet. I say "yet" because, like I said earlier, I try to see the positive side of things. I haven't given up hope. Even if the world is full of liars and cheaters who make counterfeit lip balm and fifty-dollar bills. Even if there are days I crawl under the covers and don't get up until after dark. I sincerely hope, Company T—, that you will not let me down in my request.

After years of being incommunicado, I got a letter from Joan to tell me that she was making amends with people she had harmed in the past. Step nine of a twelve-step program. She didn't apologize in the letter, so I assumed the amending needed to happen in person. She said that she'd been transferred to Montreal and insisted I come for a visit. That was Joan. Not taking *no* for an answer. But something in that note showed me she was trying and I thought, what the heck. I guess that's also the reason I didn't just hang up on your unduly supportive customer service rep. Behind all her buttery-soft lullaby talk, she was just trying to do her job.

I was unable to wear a pair of shorts or a skirt for two weeks while the skin on the front of my legs was healing. Do you know how limiting that is in July? Your customer service rep in Saudi Arabia or wherever may not realize this, but it gets hot in Toronto. Hence the purchase of the lightweight cotton pants at Winners.

It was so hot on that subway ride on my way to the airport, I thought I was going to keel over. They should invest in fans. The train wasn't full so I was able to stick my legs straight out in front of me and scissor them up and down to get some airflow up into my pant legs. I was also, thankfully, distracted with the dog sitting next to me.

What kind of person takes a dog on the subway? The little ball of fluff sitting in his owner's lap was terrified. The thing was shivering as if it were minus twenty. Who does that to a dog? An insensitive and selfish person, that's who. A person with no regard for her companion's well-being. The kind of person that should be asking herself why she has a pet in the first place. If I took Bernadette on the subway, I think her eyes might pop right out of her head.

Help me understand, Company T——, how you sleep at night knowing you are benefiting from other people's misery. Help me understand how you get away with marketing your products the way you do. Maybe I am too much of a dreamer. Taking pleasure in the misfortune of others is so deeply rooted in our society, there is a word for it. Maybe I believe too strongly in doing the right thing.

I had taken the subway to Union Station because I was flying to Montreal, a flight that Joan had paid for because, again, she had insisted and refused to let me pay. By the time I got out, my legs had really started to heat up. The Porter shuttle pick-up area was just outside the Royal York Hotel, so I went inside and found a bathroom. It was so old-fashioned and fancy that beside each of the six sinks was a decanter of mouthwash with little paper cups, a basket of individual tubes of hand cream, and some neatly stacked washcloths. I ran two washcloths under cool water and held one against each shin. Then I applied some more aloe gel, put two of the little hand creams in my purse, and left.

It must have been forty-five degrees outside as I stood there, waiting for the shuttle. To take my mind off things, I started worrying about Bernadette. I had left her with a friend of Drakkar's who claimed to be a professional dog walker. I had printed out labels with Drakkar's label maker and stuck one: "¼ CUP DRY" on her bag of dry food and the other one: "¼ CUP WET" on the can so the guy would know how much to give her. It's hard to trust anyone to do things right. I mouthed my mantra standing right there in the Porter shuttle line-up.

May I be well and happy. May I be free of conflict. May I be at peace.

I got to thinking that maybe Joan had changed. Maybe we would drink iced tea by the pool and I'd tell her how Bernadette and I take road trips up to Lake Simcoe. How we drive along the 407 in my Cavalier and Bernadette sits on my lap and looks out the window while I sing along with the easy-listening tunes they play on 98. 1 CHFI. I would tell her about my aqua-fit class at the community centre, and how I still can't lose those last five pounds because of my Nanaimo square problem. We would laugh and enjoy the sunshine like a couple of old friends.

Then I thought, maybe she hasn't changed. Maybe she bought the plane ticket to get me over there just so she could start putting me down again. Maybe she hasn't made any friends in Montreal because she's just as bossy as ever and has to lie to people like me because she's lonely. Maybe she wants to use me as a punching bag, and the whole twelve-step program is a cover. An elaborate plan, I'd have to give her that. But, of course, now I know that her recovery was just as real as me writing this letter.

May I be well and happy.

When you hear what I am about to tell you, Company T—, you might rethink that fifty-dollar Winners gift card and opt to give me a hundred dollars, or maybe a whole vacation package at someplace like The Royal York to make up for what happened next.

When I finally got to the airport terminal, I took a free *Globe and Mail* and turned straight to the horoscopes. Mine (Scorpio) read: *Resist the urge to take things too seriously today. Shift your focus to the adventure that awaits you.*

It doesn't get much clearer than that.

My legs started to itch in an unbearable way. My bag was

already checked so I had no aloe gel. I took out the individual hand creams from my purse and lifted my pant legs one at a time, applying the lotion to each one. Then it came. It felt like a hundred-thousand bee stings. A million times worse than your wax strips, believe it or not. I stood up and tried to ease the discomfort by shaking each leg like I was trying to get a pebble out of my sandal.

May I be free of conflict.

I started to deep breathe like my relaxation CD instructed and, resisting the urge to take any of it too seriously, took eight paces forward, turned, and walked back to my chair. I did this ten times. Mindful walking. I brought my awareness to the bottoms of my feet and, however slightly, the burning subsided. When I finally got on the plane, I angled that little fan thing above my head so the cold air would shoot down toward my legs.

May I be at peace.

Thanks to you, Company T—, Joan and I started our reunion off with a bunch of lies. I told her the pool party was out of the question because I was allergic to water now. I explained that I would get a rash if I went in the pool. I went so far as to bring along some Benedryl (see receipt) to make it more convincing. I wasn't about to show her my shins, striped with scabs that had started to form.

Turns out Joan's work had given her a moving allowance and she had, surprisingly, found a modest apartment instead of something modern in a nicer neighbourhood. She was living in a high-rise on Sherbrooke near Décarie, sparsely decorated with a dozen spider plants hanging from the ceiling. She said that purging was part of her healing process and she'd left most of her stuff at the Goodwill in Toronto.

"Fresh start," she said, gesturing with her arm to show off the lack of clutter. "I'm doing more with less."

I was glad she didn't choose to do without air conditioning. She wasn't wearing makeup like she used to and had gained some weight. I was surprised to see that she had a cat living with her. A big orange tabby three times the size of Bernadette was roaming around the apartment. He came over to me and sniffed at my ankles.

"Peanut is a good listener," she said. "When he wants to be."

She scratched the back of Peanut's ears. Joan tossed a crumpled piece of tinfoil, and the cat darted after it like a rocket.

"But you don't like cats," I said.

She brought out a tray of ginger cookies and topped up my glass of elderberry soda water. It tasted a bit like shampoo, but I was grateful for a cool beverage in that heat.

"Peanut's a loan," she said. "A colleague went on leave, so he's staying with me for six months."

Peanut sniffed at the cookie tray and came around to my chair. I moved my legs so he couldn't rub up against them. Joan had a few DVDs lined up on the shelf under the TV. *Eat Pray Love, The Descendants, Chocolat*, and I remembered that fateful day of the incident with your product, how I had reasoned that any kind of visual distraction might be a good thing, so I stopped in at the Movie Rack on my way home from the drugstore to pick up a DVD (the receipt I did not include). Because

Chocolat was out, I ended up getting *Iron Man 2* after taking the advice of a six-year-old fellow movie renter. I respected her honesty. As you know by now, your customer service rep did not agree with this at all.

"Sweetheart, no," she said, "You should be calm and centered, in a peaceful environment."

She sounded like a hypnotist. I could hear her shaking her head through the phone line. "This is no time to be watching an action film."

I said that I didn't think it was the movie that was the problem. She told me that next time I should put on some classical music, light a few aromatherapy candles, and drink herbal tea.

I told her there was never going to be a next time.

The good news is that back in Montreal, something positive did come out of all this. During my visit with Joan, I commented on her plants.

"I like your plants," I said.

"Even I can't kill these things," she said.

Then the dam broke and everything came spilling out. Joan started to act like a normal person. She told me about how she had decided to go to church; she didn't even believe in God, but her sponsor encouraged her to think about a higher power. She was going to every church in the city, one by one. Trying them on like a new pair of pants at Winners. "They're all so goddamned beautiful!" she said.

She was still Joan, only better.

While we sat and talked and laughed a little, it occurred to me that I was proud of her. She had set out to make changes in her life and that is exactly what she had done. People could change. Like fine print, I just needed to open my eyes wider to see it.

Peanut kept snaking his way behind my chair and pushing himself against the back of my legs, so that I had to shush him away.

"Is he bothering you?"

The burning sensation had returned.

"No, no," I said.

"Yvonne, are you okay?"

My legs were stinging so bad my eyes started to water.

"Please don't cry."

"I'm fine. Fine," I said.

I started to move my knees in and out.

"Do you need to use the bathroom?"

"No."

Both Joan and Peanut were staring at me.

"Do you want to change your clothes?" Joan asked.

I stood up and did some mindful walking. Six purposeful, heel-to-toe steps toward the kitchen, then back. I went to the balcony door and looked out at the city. There were people out there walking arm in arm, greeting each other and doing that cheek-kissing thing they do in Montreal. I went back to where Joan was sitting and slowly, slowly lifted my arms out in front of me. I held them there, open. I waited. The cat rubbed against the back of my legs, and I held my breath. Then Joan stood up and we hugged. Each of us leaned forward from the waist, no full body contact, just our shoulders touching. Pats on backs. It was a start.

So you see Company T—, there is hope for you yet.

As for Bernadette, Drakkar's friend did a good job of feeding her. When I got home, I bought Bernadette new bowls from Pet Valu. And when I asked Drakkar to borrow the label maker again he said, "Keep it, Yvonne." That's the kind of generosity of spirit I'm talking about. Genuine, honest people who do good for the sake of doing good.

In closing, I regret having to write a letter like this, Company T—, you must see that. My hope is that this letter has brought to light some things you may not have previously considered. And on behalf of all unsatisfied consumers, my goal is to give a voice to one that goes largely unheard. I feel it is my responsibility for all the people who choose to suffer in silence.

Like it or not, Company T—, we are in this together.

I anxiously await your reply to my proposal and with all due respect, I sincerely hope you make the honourable decision so that we might bring this matter to a close.

Yours truly,
Yvonne Deschamps

FASTER MILES AN HOUR

Riley walked down the long hallway to the communal kitchen with Ulrich following close behind on the worn-out carpet. The San Antonio youth hostel was dated. It looked like it hadn't been redecorated in decades. Behind the double sink was a tall window with a view of a brick wall. The room smelled used, like the duplex where her grandma had lived. Like canned vegetable soup. She put the plastic bag on the counter and kept her back to him.

"It's like we've met before," Ulrich said. His German accent stretched out the sentence, made each word elastic.

Riley picked at the knot in the plastic bag that contained their Chinese take-out. Her nails were chewed too far down to get a good hold.

"You did not just say that," she said.

Ulrich sat at the table in a gold vinyl chair that was ripped on one side where some stuffing was coming out. He cracked a can of Old Milwaukee. A patch of linoleum beside the fridge was curled up, exposing its wrinkled underbelly. Riley's teal and yellow skate shoes were covering the cigarette burns in front of the sink. Sam, the ex she left behind, would have written a song about the place in his Rocky Mountain Studio. Lyrics like, "Colliding and unknown, far from any home."

Riley kept her arms tight at her sides and hoped that Ulrich wouldn't notice her hairy armpits since she hadn't yet replaced the disposable razor she left in Puerto. She kept tugging at the knot trying to figure out where one end started and the other one ended. A plastic bag can come in handy on the road.

"Look," Ulrich said, pointing at a framed oil painting of a ship hanging on the wall beside the fridge. "Das Boot."

He laughed slow and low, sexy as raw steak. It was hardly a laugh at all. He drank his beer, his thin brown T-shirt shouting FOSTER THE PEOPLE at her. Sam had been a fan too. Riley wiped the sweat off her upper lip with the pink bandana wrapped around her wrist and glanced at Ulrich. Thick, veiny forearms. Golden-blond shaggy-dog haircut. Everything Sam wasn't. Sam looked more like an accountant than a singer-songwriter. Ulrich lifted the can and winked at her. Riley finally used a butter knife to pry the knot apart, then teased the bag open. She turned it inside out, wiped off the condensation on her skinny jeans, and hung it on the towel rack to dry.

She set the two foil containers on the table. Beef and broccoli and chicken chow mein. There were two egg rolls, still warm, in a white paper envelope soaked through with grease. Two sets of chopsticks. She opened a can of beer for herself and sat down.

"No forks?" he said.

"Fork you."

He raised his eyebrows, waited for her to say more. She scraped the chopsticks against each other as if sharpening knives, then stirred the chow mein.

"You don't know how to use chopsticks?"

Sam had shown her the technique the first time they ordered from Ginger Express and ate in her bedroom at her apartment in Canmore.

"Takes off the rough bits," she said.

"You're a bit rough."

Another wink.

He unwrapped his sticks from the paper and tapped them against each other like drumsticks.

"Tell me again, your full name?" he said.

"Louisa Mariana Antonia Miranda," Riley said.

Her black bra strap slid down onto her shoulder and hung on her arm, smirking at him. She didn't bother to fix it.

"Hold one like this," she said, "like a pen."

"To write a love poem?"

Riley punched out a short grunt of a laugh.

"And the other one just slides right in here," she said, slipping the stick into the crook of her thumb.

She had felt safe with Sam. She loved the clandestine nature of their relationship. Like being part of a secret society. "It's like we've met before." Sam had said it too, that night after the concert when they met. He said she had that kind of face that reminded people of someone else. Riley tried to offset her baby-face cheeks with thick navy eyeliner, but the effect made her look even more like a Russian doll than she already did.

She wore her dark brown hair in a shoulder length bob that she was constantly tucking behind her ears.

Riley pinched a broccoli floret and ate it. It was perfectly overcooked and extra salty. Ulrich poked and stabbed at the food. Brown sauce splashed onto the Formica tabletop. He tried and tried and tried and tried, and when she laughed, a single snort slipped out. She wiped her nose with a paper towel. Took a piece of beef in her chopsticks and held it, dripping, in front of his mouth. He went for it like a baby robin. Licked his rosy lips.

"Your tattoo," he said, talking with his mouth full. "Dragons, *ja*?"

On her eighteenth birthday, she'd had a pair of intertwined seahorses etched into the inner part of her right forearm.

"Sure," she said. "Dragons."

She wasn't going to get into it with Ulrich. She wasn't going to tell some random stranger how she had thought things were going in a very different direction with Sam when he abruptly ended their year-long affair two months ago. She had known Sam was married when they got together. It was complicated. But then he told her that he owed it to his wife. He said that he owed it to himself to stop. The handsome German in front of her didn't need to know all that. No. He didn't need to know that when Sam broke it off with Riley, she packed up everything she owned and headed south—California, Mexico, wherever. All her belongings were either in the backpack she had with her or in her Aunt Grace's basement in Kelowna. Riley wasn't about to tell this guy how her Aunt Grace had become her legal guardian when her parents were killed by a drunk driver when Riley was ten years old.

"You are the girl with the dragon tattoos," he said.

Riley raised her can in a toast and winked. "In the flesh."

She covered their unfinished chow mein with the cardboard lid and curled up the foil edges all the way around. Before she put it in the fridge, she wrote on top in blue pen: EAT ME.

"Write it in German," she said, handing him the pen.

"*Esse mich*?"

He laughed, then wrote: *Vernasche mich.*

"Savour me," he said. He put a beer in a paper bag and stuffed it down the back of his jeans. They walked for blocks, all the way downtown. Passed the funky red Torch of Friendship.

"I read about this statue," Ulrich said.

Riley slipped her arm through his as if they were an old married couple going on an after-dinner walk.

"You did not," she said.

"*Ja*, it was a gift from the Mexican government," he said, stroking the top of her hand lightly, lightly. "The two parts are twisted up like that because relationships can be complicated."

Strands of thousands of tiny white lights lined the streets of the old city. Palm trees drooped in the glow. They stopped walking. She looked up at him and his eyes sparkled like bits of blown glass. She stood on her tiptoes for an oyster sauce-flavoured kiss. It was still weird kissing lips that weren't Sam's.

They sat on a concrete monument across from the Alamo, legs outstretched, thighs touching. He ran his fingertips up her arm. A slice of moon hung over the old grey building. It hung there in contradiction, cradling her confusion and at the same time encouraging her. Traffic hummed around them. A siren howled. He touched the shiny black pendant that hung on a strip of leather around her neck.

"I like this," he said.

"Black coral."

She nestled into his side like a kitten. He smelled like bread. She put a hand under his shirt. He moved the leather cord to the side and kissed her neck all the way around. *Vernasche mich.* They stayed like this until, fully charged, they went back to her room.

The next morning, he was asleep when she left. She rolled up his T-shirt, shoved it into her backpack, and threw away the bit of paper bag on which he had written his email. On the sidewalk in front of the hostel, she re-wrapped the pink bandana around her wrist. Seven a.m., and the half empty streets were already baking under the Texan sun.

Riley took a window seat near the back of the city bus and watched the lives of others. A man in a suit buying a newspaper. A group of uniformed school kids, one dragging a stick along the curb. The steeple of a brick church painted white, poking the sky like a dart. Sam had been her anchor. When she spun herself up into a storm of what-ifs, they would go for a hike and he'd sing Billy Bragg songs to her. He would say things like, "Remember what's good."

Puerto Escondido had been good. Ulrich was good. She was filling herself with experiences, but she was hollow without Sam. What if she turned back? What if she just showed up at his house and announced herself? What if.

The bus stopped a block beyond the address she'd scrawled on the palm of her left hand. She doubled back and passed a warehouse with a lot of broken windows. At a take-out pizza place, a five-foot-tall decal of a grinning tomato with pepperoni eyes smiled at her. She clenched her stomach while she walked, tried to make the void inside her go away. Tried to turn this hot Texas morning into an authentic adventure, a story to tell later, when she had someone to tell.

The place looked like a poorly aging body, unkempt and frail. Faded green paint was shredded in parts, burned by the sun. Judging by the wooden shingle hanging out front on a rusted chain, it had been years since the two-storey house had been an insurance office. The building looked ready to exhale. Other than the outdated sign, there was nothing to indicate that it was even the right address. Riley double-checked her palm, felt for the Swiss Army knife in her pocket, and walked the gravel driveway like a gangplank.

She reached for the iron ring on the door and got a whiff of beef and broccoli mixed with Hawaiian ginger body mist when she lifted her arm. She wiped the sweat from her forehead with the bandana and tucked her hair behind her ears. A dry strip of paint stuck out and she picked at it, peeled it off the wall, flicked it onto the grass. A warm wind sent goose bumps up her arms, and she felt her neck for the piece of black rock.

No one answered at A-1 Drive Away. She tried the door and it opened.

"Hello?" she said.

Even on a sunny day like today, the entrance was dark and

musty. A small window made of glass bricks on the side of the staircase let in a single stream of light. Tiny dust particles floated in the air. There was a tin canister sitting on an old wooden table pushed against the far wall. A black umbrella leaned up in the corner. More lyrics for Sam.

A voice called, "Up here."

She started up the stairs. Each step a new fear. Sam would love this uncertainty. The wood was uneven under her weight, and one of the steps buckled so much she thought she might fall right through. What if she did? What if she fell onto a pile of dead bodies? Skeletons of all the kidnapped travellers that had come before her, wanting cheap rides. This was Texas. Shady state troopers and chainsaw massacres. Stop it stop it stop it stop it stop it. Shut up. Shut. This. Down. Riley reached up and swept at a cobweb. She sneezed and kept going. The drive-away was cheaper than a bus, and the more she saved getting to Grace's friend's place in Clearwater, the longer she could stay. She couldn't let that free condo go to waste. For once in her life she was going to have a taste of luxury. She took another step. What if she got abducted or raped or murdered? She could get tied to a chair and beaten and tortured for information she didn't have. She could have her limbs removed one by one. Stupid stupid stupid. Get out get out get out. She could be skinned, maybe eaten alive! Maybe flown to Turkey and forced into sexual slavery for an affluent Prince-in-waiting because a fake profile on a black-market, sex-trade website had been created using her photo.

She smacked her own cheek three times, fast. The hollowness

inside her was turning to openness. She had learned early on in life that the journey was hers alone. And then Sam. What they had was so wrong, it was right. She felt like they couldn't be touched; she felt strong with him, protected. Secrecy was their ally, their shield.

Riley took one last foolish step, and at the top of the stairs entered an office that reeked of cigars and Old Spice. The room contained a desk, two outdoor patio chairs, a black filing cabinet, and a very large man. The walls were the colour of piss. The floors, a darker shade of piss. The big guy behind the desk wore a short-sleeved plaid shirt and suspenders and looked like he weighed about 400 pounds. The desk was stacked with papers and folders. He lowered his reading glasses and peered at her over the rims.

"I called yesterday," Riley said. "You got some cars that need to go to Florida?"

"Ah," he said, and motioned for her to sit in one of the plastic chairs in front of the desk. "I'm Ronnie."

She put her backpack on the floor and sat down. She showed Ronnie her passport, signed some documents, and gave him a $200 cash deposit. While Big Ronnie did the paperwork, Riley tucked her hair behind her ears and picked at a hangnail on her thumb.

Back in Puerto, Riley had taken two pimply faced British girls to Tequila Bum Bum—pronounced "boom boom," which she learned, after much teasing and laughter, early on in her stay— the town's beachfront disco, for New Year's Eve. The Brits had arrived at Hotel Aster that morning and were punchy from jet lag. Over distorted Bob Marley music, Riley introduced the girls to the locals she had befriended—Carmen and Pato, Miguel—in the last two months of living in the secluded Mexican town. Outside the club, the tide was rolling over itself on the dark beach less than fifty feet away. Fishing boats were tied to palm trees, and chunks of driftwood were scattered along the shore like pieces of abstract art. Her impulse was to send Sam an email, write him a postcard. Do the impossible. In Puerto, she fell asleep to the sound of the surf and woke up in the middle of the night sweaty and guilty after dreaming about other guys.

Riley wore her signature white tank top and black bra and a pair of white wrap-around cotton pants. A long loop of iridescent pink shells hung around her neck, a gift from Ingrid for helping clean rooms at the hotel.

"*Amigas*," Miguel shouted. "*Vamos bailar!*"

"Bloody brilliant way to spend New Year's Eve," one of the British girls said.

"It's so warm," said the other. "In December!"

Even though he was drunk on tequila, Miguel's laugh was boisterous and raspy from years of seducing tourists who passed through town. He had tried with Riley, but since she had stuck around they had become pals. On the dance floor, Miguel sandwiched himself between the drunk foreigners. Forehead against forehead, they swayed this way and that to R.E.M.'s "Shiny Happy People."

Vaquero was Miguel's younger brother. Seventeen years younger. Carmen had told Riley stories. Vaquero had spent time in jail on an assault charge. There were drugs. He rarely went out in public. His name meant "cowboy." Riley had seen him just once before; three weeks after she arrived, she'd seen his limping figure at the far end of the beach. It was early in the morning, and there was a rugged patch of coral among the rocks where the surf got rough. She had been warned about the undertow, and danger signs were erected in the sand. *Cuidado, fuerte corriente!* Take care, strong riptide! Vaquero limped because of his hoof. Miguel told the story one afternoon while they were playing shuffleboard.

"Lost his foot, poor kid," Miguel said, slapping the inside of his ankle so hard that his flip-flop fell off. "Running in the field with the horses."

As a teen, Vaquero had contracted a bacterial infection that usually only affected farm animals. His foot was amputated from the ankle down, and a doctor in Oaxaca had attached the hoof. Vaquero walked with a cane at first.

"We made a booth behind the cabanas," Miguel said, shaking his head as he explained how they tried to help their mom pay off some of the medical bills. "Charged ten pesos a look."

On the dance floor back at the disco, Riley danced with her hands up over her head as if she was in a smoky, wavy trance. She traced the outline of her own body, her sides and hips, shook her head from side to side. Then, like an apparition that had crawled out of the sea, Vaquero silently appeared on the dance floor. He was shirtless, cut like steel, a strand of red and brown beads around his neck. He had mastered the use of the hoof; it was hardly noticeable and he moved gracefully, sliding and sweeping over the laminate floor as if he were in some kind of tribal ritual. He slid up behind Riley, and his tangled black mane fell across her shoulders. She caught the scent of coconut oil. Vaquero took her hand in his as if he had done it a thousand times before and led her down to the beach. She ached for Sam's hands, one last time; Sam's touch, which calmed her. Sam had been the turning point, the catalyst that had allowed her fear to dissolve. On the nights he left her and went home, he would put his hands on her face and press his forehead against hers and count for a full ten seconds. It was this gesture that, in her final moments before sleep, made her realize that she needed him much more than she had wanted to.

The moon was high and full and lit up the beach. Barefoot on the sand, she followed Vaquero past the boats, past the driftwood. It was impossible not to look down at the hoof that burrowed its way through the sand, digging as if it had a mind of its own. At the edge of the water, he took off his shorts and stood naked in front of her. She focused on a deep scar below his left nipple, four inches long, that stood out in the moonlight. He lifted Riley's tank top up and over her head. The shells hung down between her breasts. He didn't touch her bra but pulled the tie at the front of her pants, then tossed them onto the beach. They waded into the water.

"You like me a little bit?" Vaquero asked. His voice sounded damaged, like an old rock star's.

He moved her in front of him, his hands on her waist, coaxing her forward until they were waist-deep in the ocean, the line in the water where warm meets cold. Riley had already had a few tequila shots. She wiggled her toes in the sand back and forth, making grooves that quickly filled with water.

"Sure, I like you," she said, turning to look at him.

He had dark, almond-shaped eyes, like an Indian. She hadn't spoken to him before. He never joined the rest of them in shuffleboard or darts in the afternoons. Never played beach volleyball at dusk. She felt like she was on the edge of a cliff looking into an abyss. Waves lapped at her ribs. She flexed her thighs. Far beyond, the deepest water was folding and swirling, undulating in the vast undercurrent, terror lingering on the surface.

Something in his fist flashed in the moonlight. A leather cord, a necklace with a black oval pendant on it.

"*Para ti,*" he said.

His eyes were alive, brown-black in the moonlight. He put the necklace over her head and placed his entire hand over the pendant on her chest, the shells jingling from his touch. Everything was in constant motion. She brought her hands to his face and was surprised at how soft it was.

"*Gracias,*" she said.

He lifted the pendant to his lips, then to the sky. Held it there for a moment then placed it back on her chest.

"*Luna de fuego.*"

He kissed her then, hard and fiery. Her first kiss since Sam. Hidden. Forbidden. Her stomach flipped. They were in the water up to their necks. Years later, when Riley found herself stuck in an office job staring at a screensaver of palm trees and a white sandy beach, she would remember this. He licked the outline of her mouth. Kissed her again, softer this time. Everything was salty. The Mexican beast pulled her into his naked chest, and the tide receded under the great ball of the moon, the same moon that had eclipsed the sun, an event she had watched with Sam. It was the same moon that had hung low in the sky on the night of her parents' funeral. Vaquero took one hand and pressed the heel of his palm against her pubic bone. Then lower. Slid his hand further down and cupped her under the water. He was sculpting her with one hand while the other circled around her back. He lifted her body, buoyant in the water, and she hooked her heels around the back of his thighs. She didn't resist when he submerged them both underwater. No one to save her from a descent into darkness. She was a mermaid now, dancing with a wild seahorse. She linked her arms tight around his neck and clung to him. There was no sound underwater; it was muffled and insulated, as if they were in a cave. Everything was liquefying. She might very well implode and melt into the sea. Thump thump, thump thump. Was it the hoof? Her heart beating?

Vaquero straightened his legs, and they broke through the surface of the water. Boney M singing "Auld Lang Syne" in the distance.

Under they went again. A second baptism. A dare? An offering to the sea gods? Father, son, and holy shit she needed air. She kicked her legs and felt his teeth clamp onto her collarbone. His hands were on her shoulders pressing, pressing. A violin squealed. She was convulsing, writhing, reaching. She needed saving, now! A drumbeat, base and carnal. Fuck you, Sam. She had learned this behaviour from him. She was drowning because of him. What if she died out here in the sea with a cloven-hoofed Mexican convict? Happy freaking New Year! Time was running out. He gripped her hips, vice-lock hands squeezing tight, tighter, and then lifted her into thin air. The moon was still there. The music. She lay back and floated. It was so clear. Sharp as cut glass. How had she not seen all these stars before? She was unsinkable. She leveraged herself in the water and caught a glimpse of him leaving her in the moonlight. A silent cowboy swimming out to sea without a horse. Alone again. The moon her only witness.

Back at A-1 Drive Away, Big Ronnie continued sorting through papers in his smelly office.

"You'll get this back at the dealership in Lakeland," he said, nodding at the $200 on the desk.

Sam would have gone along with this whole thing, no problem. He wouldn't have even asked for a receipt.

"Don't I get a receipt or something?"

"You'll get cash in Lakeland. Keep your gas receipts."

The room was warm, but Ronnie wasn't sweating. The stench of anticipation and cigar weighted the air. There was a small window, closed and half-covered with a piece of cardboard. What if she ran? Her money was sitting right there. She could grab it and bolt. Take the stairs two at a time and keep running. Take the bus to Clearwater and be done with it.

There was a mousetrap on the floor by the filing cabinet. She scanned the rest of the room, found one in every corner. Riley dabbed her upper lip with the bandana.

"You got mouse trouble?" she said.

"Rats," Ronnie said, still writing.

Gorging on all those rotting bodies in the cellar under the stairs, no doubt. There was no food in the traps.

"Peanut butter sometimes works," she said. It was something her Aunt Grace did. Hopefully, something she still did. Hopefully, her stuff wasn't infested with a bunch of mouse crap.

Ronnie raised his eyes at her without moving his head. She nodded, then shrugged.

Ulrich was probably wondering where his T-shirt was by now. Maybe he found that plastic bag she forgot on the towel rack. Suddenly there was a heavy clunking sound outside the office, and a man entered the room with a cigar the size of a small banana in his mouth. He was the same stature as Ronnie, maybe even taller, and also wearing a short-sleeved plaid shirt and suspenders. He dropped two folders on the desk and spoke past the cigar through yellow teeth.

"Hi, I'm Ronnie," he said.

The new Ronnie looked at Riley. Riley looked at the first Ronnie. The first Ronnie continued with his paperwork. Right. Okay. This was cool. This was totally and completely not weird. What if she ran now? There was still time.

"Hey," Riley said.

"She's for Florida," said the first Ronnie.

"Cars are out back," said the second Ronnie.

She followed the second Ronnie down the hall to the back of the house. He pointed to four cars parked in a fenced yard. A silver four-door Buick, a white station wagon, a dirty truck, and a gleaming red sports car.

"Your pick," he said.

The Porsche 911 Turbo was a two-seater with a rear engine, so she stuffed her backpack under the hood and ignored the fact that 800 pounds of Ronnies had just handed her the keys to a very shiny, very expensive car with Florida plates so that she, a woman with a Canadian passport, could drive the car through Texas and Louisiana on a three-day delivery to Florida. She got in the car, started the engine. She turned on the radio and an ad for San Antonio's Q101.9 iHeartRadio station came on, followed by a half-country, half-pop tune she'd never heard of, and she let out a belly laugh from deep in her gut. Riley felt the pendant around her neck, put her sunglasses on, and shifted the car into first gear.

Since New Year's, she had gotten used to walking on the beach at dawn, and on her last day in Puerto, she had taken one final early-morning stroll. The rising sun created a path from the rocks to the open water, an infinite line of floating sequins. She walked the length of the beach secretly hoping to see Vaquero one last time, but no one was out at that hour. Riley stripped down to nothing but the pendant, swam out into the ocean under a cloudless coastal sky. Solace. She would miss the quiet haunting of the sea. Beneath the surface, her movements sounded like the softest kind of cymbals crashing, faintly, faintly dissolving into nothing.

She floated on her back with her arms out at her sides. With time, the beauty of anything morphs into an echo of itself. It becomes a shadow, a memory, like this moment. There were days when Sam was still fully there, almost as if he were there next to her. Other times, like now, he was fading, being diluted. She began to tread water, keeping only her head above the surface, and saw the surfers start to emerge from their cabanas at the other end of the beach.

She met her posse of friends for a goodbye breakfast before she caught the bus to Oaxaca and then on to Mexico City. A fiesta of *café con leche* and hotcakes *con frutas* on the beach until they switched to beer and downed half a dozen Coronas before noon. She slept all the way to Mexico City.

Riley met Doug at the Casa de Cambio line-up inside the main bus terminal. Doug was from Vancouver, six-foot-four, and smelled like cucumber soap. He said "hey" at the beginning or end of every sentence. She had a four-hour layover before her bus left for San Antonio, so they installed themselves in orange bucket seats in a corner of the terminal.

"Hey, I gotta kill seven hours," Doug had said.

He was a nursing student at the university, heading to Puerto Escondido for a surfing holiday. They shared a bag of lime-salted peanuts and a couple of cans of Tecate. She undid the bandana from her wrist and rubbed suntan lotion on her arms.

"You got a sweet tan, hey," Doug said.

He offered to take her pulse and put three fingers just below her wrist on the inside of her right arm.

"Hey," he said, noting her tattoos, "wicked ink."

She chewed on the cuticle of her index finger while he watched the second hand on his watch. When he finished, he held her hand a little longer than necessary and told her that her heart rate was "awesome, hey."

"Excellent bedside manner," she said.

Doug had grown up in North Vancouver and did a lot of skateboarding as a kid. He'd learned to surf in Nanaimo and lifted the pant leg of his cargo pants to show off a scar that ran the length of his left shin, a souvenir from a spill when he was a beginner. She touched it like it was wet paint. He took out a small container of Blistex and rubbed some on the scar.

"It gets dry sometimes, hey."

She grabbed the lip balm from him and applied some to her lips. Sam used to massage her face with sweet almond oil and clary sage; he would do this while she lay in bed wearing one of his T-shirts. He'd massage her face, then while she pretended to be asleep, he'd lift up her shirt and rub the rest of her body with the scented oil. He said it was balancing.

Riley told Doug about Puerto. How to pronounce Tequila Bum Bum, where they played beach volleyball at dusk, and the address of Hotel Aster. When she warned him about the undertow, he said, "It's not my first rodeo, hey."

They hooked up in a stall in the public bathroom, and it was cramped and vigorous. After, she pocketed the Blistex. Sam would have been jealous of Doug. Doug was the opposite of Vaquero. And it was good with Doug because of both of those things.

Riley sped along in the little red car on the Interstate passing roadside diners and Mobil gas stations. A highway billboard read: "Lone Star Gun Shop, 4 miles ahead." Crumpled up heaps of rusted out junk—machinery and broken car parts— were abandoned along the side of the highway, piled twenty feet high in places. The landscape was a disappointment, a complete contrast to her dreamy preconceived notion of looming mountains and deserts filled with cactus plants. Like the rubber cactus gag-gift she had anonymously mailed to Sam when she first got to Texas. She'd signed the card, "To a real prick." He could have left his wife. What if he had? What if he was here now? He'd be playing his guitar, hair blowing in the wind, singing along with the radio. But he was too much of a chicken. A chicken who made a choice, who crossed the road, then turned around and went back home.

The car might as well have been carved from gold. She had never driven something as fast. Passing other cars was a breeze. It was like being on her own private racetrack. She got through Houston, Lafayette, and Baton Rouge, all before sunset. She was making good time. Her Aunt Grace always liked it when they made "good time" on a trip. No delays, no hiccups, no accidents. Riley was making such good time that she decided to stop in Pensacola for onion rings and beer.

On the edge of town, she entered a dusty bar with bronze imprints of coyotes painted on wood-panelled walls. A neon-pink silhouette of Elvis stitched on black velvet was tacked above the jukebox. The place smelled like over-used cooking oil and neglect.

A woman wearing a black shirt, blue jeans, and tan boots interrupted Riley's dart game. She introduced herself as Silver.

Said that she and the gals, a team of competitive arm wrestlers, were having a party later.

"I got a farmhouse fifteen miles from here," Silver said, thumb dangling from her belt loop. Silver's friend, a taller woman with greasy brown curls, moved closer to Riley.

"This here is Angie," Silver said.

"I'm just passing through," said Riley.

"We can see that," Angie said, revealing a substantial space between her two front teeth.

Two more women—more denim, more boots—gathered at the dartboard. The jukebox made shuffling noises, then stopped. Angie snaked in and stood too close to Riley. Her curls hung heavy; they needed a wash. The jukebox started up again. Johnny Cash, "Solitary Man."

"I should get going," Riley said, moving toward her stool at the bar.

"What's the hurry?" Angie said.

She put one hand on either side of the bar, pinning Riley against the edge. Close up, the pores in Angie's nose were little craters filled with black. Riley stopped herself from reaching out to squeeze one.

"I have to use the bathroom," Riley said.

She took a step to her left and Angie blocked her.

"Whatcha got there? Good-luck charm?" Angie said, touching the piece of black coral at Riley's neck. Her lips looked like two elastic bands pulled taut. Riley moved right. Angie blocked her again.

"Where you from?" Angie said, her breath rank as sour milk.

"North Dakota."

"You a long way from home, girl," Silver said.

Riley cleared her throat. Her last two cold onion rings sat in a wicker basket on the bar. A couple of pieces of deep-fried bad luck. A memory hit her like an electric shock: Sam making home-made onion rings in her cast-iron frying pan, back in her Canmore apartment, while she sat cross-legged on a kitchen chair, scrolling through his iPod, making selections while he cooked.

"You look thirsty," Angie said.

Angie reached behind Riley's back and picked up her pint of beer that was still half full. Angie pressed the glass to Riley's mouth so hard that Riley was forced to tilt her head back as Angie lifted the drink. Riley swallowed and some beer dribbled onto the front of her tank top. Riley wiped her face with her bandana, looked Angie in the eye, and winked.

"My car is out back. Which way to the farm?"

Silver got a pen from the barmaid and drew the way to the farm on a napkin. It looked like a twisted timeline, mapping out Riley's future.

"Cool," Riley said. "But I still need to use the bathroom."

Angie ran her hand down the back of Riley's shirt and pinched her just below the ribs. Riley took Angie's hand. It was small, like a child's, with chipped, dirty fingernails. She brought it up to her cheek.

"Moon fire," she said. *Luna de fuego.*

Angie shook free from Riley's grip. Riley pulled a dart from the corkboard behind her and flicked the plastic end with her finger, making a flapping noise. Angie lunged forward and closed her fist around the dart, around Riley's hand. She leaned in and kissed Riley. A high school kiss. Truth or dare? Oh, if Sam could see her now. Riley suppressed a laugh. Her mouth mashed against Angie's elastic band lips. Of all the kisses she'd had, this was the saddest; it was like kissing her own hand as a teenager, trying to get it right. She released the muscles in her jaw and thought of Vaquero, Doug, Ulrich, an effortless and impossible collection of kisses. Sam, too—effortless and impossible. Riley kissed back. It was repulsive and lustful, and as Angie backed off, a rival gang of competitive arm wrestlers entered the bar for last call.

The gang of women, dressed in costume, stood tall, inflated from a recent victory. They moved leisurely and confidently, like creatures of the night, panthers tracking prey. Raggedy Ann had red woolly braids and smoky eyes. There was a sexy prison matron in fishnet stockings and a tight navy dress tapping a billy club against her palm. Two Cher look-alikes and a peroxide blonde Cinderella in clear plastic clogs crowded around a table. They sat down and gave each other high fives as Raggedy Ann approached the bar.

"Evening, Miss Silver," she said. "You gonna buy us a celebration drink or what?"

"Or what," Silver said.

Angie had stepped away from Riley and took her place beside Silver. The other two women stood on her other side. Riley inched her way toward the bathroom.

"Oh, that's right," Raggedy Ann said. "Y'all didn't qualify for the tournament."

She made an exaggerated frown with her smudged red lip-stick. She did a small hop-skip in front of the dartboard and lifted both hands in the air, palms open. "There's always next year, right?"

Cinderella carried the trophy, a plank of wood with a brass forearm mounted on it. The hand was curled into a tight fist, the middle finger sticking straight up. The whole thing was spray-painted in look-at-me gold.

"Truce?" Raggedy Ann said to Silver. Then to the barmaid, "Blood Clots all around!"

Riley made it a few inches closer to the bathroom. Within moments, a tray of reddish orange Jell-O shots in little white paper cups appeared on the bar. Cinderella started handing them out. Raggedy Ann spotted Riley.

"Who's this?" she asked Silver.

"She's with me," Angie said, taking a shooter from Cinderella and handing it to Riley. Angie slurped the shot back in one swallow.

"Congratulations," Riley said.

"Oh, doll face, you ain't from 'round here, are you?"

"We're leaving," Silver said.

"We ain't scared you outta your own home again, now did we?" Raggedy Ann said. "How we ever gonna get along if you keep running off like this?"

Silver crushed the shooter and red goop oozed through her fingers onto the floor. Riley took baby steps backwards. Angie went to the dartboard and pulled out the rest of the darts. Held them up in her little clenched fists like daggers.

"Why you gotta be like that?" Silver said to Raggedy Ann.

Raggedy Ann batted her grotesquely fake eyelashes.

"Who, me?"

Angie moved closer to Raggedy Ann. Silver threw her crumpled cup at the wall.

"Why don't we wrestle over who's gonna take that pretty little thing home tonight?" Raggedy Ann planted her elbow on the bar and gave Silver a wave with her stubby fingers.

Riley made a beeline for the trophy, scooped it, and ran for her life, out of the bar and to the car. She started the engine and drove into the night as fast as the little red sports car would take her. She drove with the headlights off until she reached the outskirts of the other side of town and pulled into the back parking lot of a 7-Eleven. She downed a carton of orange juice and slept in the car. At dawn, she washed her face and armpits in the store's bathroom and bought coffee and a three-pack of chocolate cupcakes, icing sugar squiggled across each one. She got back on the Interstate-10 East, the fuck-you trophy riding in the passenger seat beside her.

She had pictured a transformation. A trip down the rabbit hole, into lemon groves and the Everglades, but the idea of a road trip was more romantic than the actual trip itself. It wasn't flashy or exotic, it was plain; it was farmland and birch trees. The scenery was no different than what she could have seen back home. If it wasn't for a few orange orchards popping up every few miles, it could have been a regular sunny day anywhere in southern Alberta.

Maybe it didn't need to be fantastical or foreign. Maybe it

just needed to be somewhere else, somewhere that showed her there were other ways to live. Thank you, Pensacola. Thank you, Ulrich. Thank you, Doug, Puerto, Vaquero. *Muchas gracias a todos los jalapeños!* Thank you, Sam, for the standard you set, the example of intimacy that can occur between predator and prey.

Fifteen minutes outside the Tallahassee city limits, she reached an open stretch of road, long and straight as black licorice. Windows down, sunroof open, farms flashed by like staccato notes. More cowboy country music on the radio, whooping and yee-hawing. She turned up the volume.

Riley felt the coral pendant at her neck. She applied pressure to it with her thumb against her forefinger. It broke. It wasn't coral at all. It was a piece of plastic with a hole drilled through the top. She leaned over and opened the glove box. Got out the Swiss Army Knife. Steering the car with her knees, she held the sharp edge away from her neck, and sawed through the leather strap. The pendant dropped on the seat beside her and landed next to the gleaming golden fist. She picked up the broken bit of plastic and tossed it out the sunroof.

"Yee haw!"

She accelerated. Riley extended her arms all the way forward and pushed back against the seat. Sand eroded beneath her toes and slipped away. She felt feverish.

"YEEE HAWWWW!"

She accelerated.

She gripped the wheel tighter, her face flush. She shook her hair from side to side, wild as a stallion. The speedometer crept up to the 100-mph mark. The speed was paralyzing in its purity, the movement clear and sharp and sweet.

She accelerated.

Somewhere, waves were crashing into rock, a dart was heading towards a bull's-eye, Raggedy Ann was tonguing Cinderella. Somewhere, a songwriter was making breakfast for his wife, writing lyrics in his mind about a girl he once knew.

She accelerated.

There is a line between danger and terror that is like biting into human flesh, a finger or forearm. Teeth sinking into a shoulder, searching for bone, consumed by need. A dotted line where risk meets reverence and fear dissolves. The speedometer reached 130 and the road lay ahead like a tightrope. Deliberate and controlled, she veered the car gainfully, derisively, to the left.

She accelerated.

LANDING AREA

Not baby blue, not sea-foam green, not even close to what she
was trying to achieve. Colleen pushed her brush with some
force into the bottom of the Mason jar full of cloudy water and
squished it flat on both sides. The top half of the canvas was
covered in a sickly blue; it looked tacky and manufactured. She
wrapped the brush in a rag and squeezed out the water, rub-
bing the bristles between her fingers. On a piece of plywood, she
started with a fresh dollop of white and added equal parts violet
grey and ultramarine. The paint looked grossly edible, like icing
on birthday cake. A cake that someone like Lila would buy.

She got up and refilled her MEC water container from the
jug that sat on top of the bar fridge. The ceramic duck with the
chipped beak was staring back at her from the windowsill.

"What's up, duck?" she said.

In the early afternoon light, the thing was the same colour as
a freezer-burnt Creamsicle. Its heavily lashed lids were forever
stuck open. She had carried the thing around with her for years,
and now it stared at her, judging her. The clouds shifted outside,
and the colour of the duck changed to a muted butterscotch.
The thing had as much feeling as a bowl of pudding.

Colleen and Mark lived in a twelve-by-twenty-foot rectangular structure that sat back among the trees on Mark's brother's property on British Columbia's Sunshine Coast. Mark had built the place with Gary's help, using scrap lumber from the mill a few kilometres inland from Madeira Park where Gary worked. A few weeks ago, Mark picked up a couple of morning shifts at the mill, and they hadn't got around to finishing the window casings yet. She expected them home at any minute.

There was a ladder next to the wash basin leaning against a crossbeam that supported the loft where they slept. The bar fridge was plugged into a power bar attached to an extension cord that ran all the way out to Gary's shop. Also plugged into the power bar was a cord that snaked around the ceiling, ending in a naked bulb that hung above Mark's reading chair. Colleen's easel, a stool, and a bookshelf took up the rest of the living space.

Colleen took turns with Lila, Gary's wife, getting groceries from the IGA in the nearby town of Sechelt. When it was Lila's turn, Colleen would give her a list of things she needed. Whole canned tomatoes, navy beans, celery. Lila would return with diced tomatoes and kidney beans and carrots and Colleen was never sure if it was spite or stupidity when Lila never got it right.

Colleen stood in front of the painting. It was the worst kind of blue. Auntie's Cardigan Blue. It was supposed to be a rendering of the clean mountain air, of air free of traffic and transit and dumpsters, air so fresh it could kill you. Out here, there were no windows to peer into and catch a slice of drama or movement.

There was no people-watching, just the restlessness of unfinished business that manifested itself in a useless painting. When Mark wasn't there, it was just her and an opinionated, mute duck.

"Say it," she said to the duck. "Tell me how it sucks ass."

They had decided to make the move in January, get through the worst of it first. Give it a year. She got her absence approved by her supervisor at the art school to take the year off from teaching. Colleen had a show at a gallery on Granville Island the following spring, and living on the Sunshine Coast would give her time to finish the pieces she needed. It would give Mark the peace of mind his sponsor suggested. Less temptation, triggers, access.

Their last night in Vancouver, Mark and Colleen had a meal at the Liliget Feast House. They ordered fried bannock and maple-smoked salmon. The dimly lit dining room was romantic in a Romanesque kind of way, with buffed wooden pillars two feet thick that separated the place into sections. The tables were designed in such a way that a slab of wood had to be lifted to climb into the plank seats. The floor was covered with little rocks from the beach, and large black and red Haida prints hung on the stone walls.

"I put birdseed out for the sparrows in the alley," he said. Two fingers tapping alternately on the thick wooden tabletop. She covered his hand with hers. "But the crows got to it first."

"You can't control nature."

Under the table, Colleen moved the pebbles at her feet with her shoe. Mark nodded. He took a drink of his sparkling water.

"How are you feeling?" Colleen said.

She tore off a piece of the puffy bannock bread. It reminded her of a doughnut.

"Like a dried-up conifer," he said, running his fingers though his thick hair, overdue for a cut.

"We can always come back if it doesn't work," she said.

Mark peeled the armour-like silver skin off a strip of dried salmon.

"The fish used to be better here."

"Why don't you try the soup?"

Mark took her hand across the table, lifted it to his face, kissed her palm.

"This is what *we* want, right?" he said.

She ran her thumb along the line of his jaw and down to his chin. The two days' stubble felt like the low-grade sand paper she kept in her workbox to smooth out the edges of her frames. The scratchy hair would be rough on her face later, but it wouldn't matter. His chin rough on her thighs, marking her with a rash.

"Of course."

Steph knew the base order never changed: whisky, pot, porn. Sometimes the loggers added cartons of cigarettes or a case of Big Red gum. Coffee Crisp bars and Werther's Originals for the rotten sweet tooth of the foreman at the camp. Today's delivery included a dozen packages of beef jerky and some shrink-wrapped Pepperettes. Fly the supplies in, take the money out; a good old-fashioned bootlegging operation. They paid Steph

1,200 bucks a trip to ship in whatever they wanted, and as long as it fit in her Cessna and wasn't explosive she couldn't care less what was in the cardboard boxes. Cargo was cargo.

The wide river snaked its way through the forest below, and the great navy ocean stretched out to the west. The forecast had called for scattered clouds, a low ceiling that was already at 5,000 feet. Clearcutting hadn't affected this area yet. Soon enough, the destruction would come and people would start living in denial amidst the disintegration. Or they'd move. Not Steph. She accepted the loggers' money and didn't watch the news. She didn't have long days anymore. Now her days were just the right length.

Damned if she was going to end up resentful. A bitter old lesbian filing the calluses on her palms with the pumice stone Daisy kept in a ceramic planter with her *InStyle* magazines beside the tub. Steph was not about to waste the rest of her thirties grooming her marred hands that had seen a shit-ton of garden work she wasn't even interested in. Hoeing the same rows of snap peas in the same garden season after season without wearing gloves with the nubby grips on them like Daisy always told her to wear.

"When are you going to clean out that bird bath?" Daisy would nag.

Daisy did contract work as a makeup artist and often got invited to film industry events. They would hire a sitter for Brooke, and attend the cocktail parties that followed when production wrapped for some made-for-TV movie. Steph would drink beer and stand around plates of shucked oysters sitting in trays of melting ice. She often ended up talking to the construction crew, learned their trade secrets, like how to build bookcases out of Styrofoam.

"Don't believe half of what you see," a grip told her.

"And none of what you hear," the sound tech said.

They laughed and ate, and across the room Daisy drank her gin and tonics, one after the other, trying to secure her next gig.

"Better to be a dreamer than a liar, I guess," Steph said.

"What?" the grip said.

"Beer?" she said.

"Sure," said the sound guy.

It had been a year since she had woken up knowing that she would rather be alone than go one more day feeling an anvil in her gut, a feeling so heavy it could have anchored her there, if she gave in. She would miss their daughter, Brooke, of course, but she needed to fly.

Colleen put her brush down and shook the container of gesso like it was a can of coconut milk for a full minute. The blue was still off. The combination of violet grey and ultramarine created a flattened slate colour. She took the widest brush from her wicker basket of supplies, dipped it in the white goop, and painted over the whole hideous thing.

"There," she said to the duck.

Colleen approached the figurine. Leaned in and faced it, eye to eye. Fine lines like rivulets spread out from under the beak where the paint was cracked. Maybe she should paint the duck blue. Reconstruct the beak with papier-mâché. Give it new eyes and eyelashes. She touched her nose to the broken beak. It moved a little. It was hollow and hardly weighed a thing. An excruciating silence between them. A staring contest. If the duck could speak, what would it say? *You think painting over it is going to fix it?*

For bathing and washing clothes, they kept a hefty cast-iron pot on the wood-burning stove. Last night, it was so dark when she came in from the outhouse that she ran right into the door jam and cracked the arm of her glasses. Lila could offer to let them use *her* bathroom, but she doesn't.

Mark and Gary should have been home by now. Colleen was anxious. She'd been sleeping too soundly here. Mark was sleeping better too, and she couldn't tell if it was the kind of help he needed. But this is what they had agreed on. Space, time, a place to paint. A place for Mark to continue his recovery. But the rectangle was so cramped, she didn't feel inspired. She was too busy daydreaming about Thai restaurants and outdoor markets and the studios back at the school.

A few nights ago, she'd dreamed she was pregnant. With her swollen abdomen she climbed up to the loft and gave birth to two electric guitars. Preemies. Their necks were abnormal, skinny and too short. They were made from hard wood, maybe oak or walnut, and cords stuck out from the bottom of the guitars that weren't attached to anything. The image had left her unsettled.

She pulled the faded red scarf she had been using as a head-band down to her neck and pushed her greasy hair behind her ears. The scarf was a generic cotton fabric, thin from overuse, with a strand of silver woven into it. She'd bought it in Portugal years ago on a backpacking trip through Europe.

The gesso had to set, so Colleen pulled her hiking boots over her wool socks and went outside. There was no need for gloves or a hat. She wore a fleece vest over one of Mark's grey long-sleeved T-shirts.

On the way to the outhouse, Colleen took a few steps in place to listen to the crunchy mess beneath her boots. A painting of the ground seemed more attainable than her attempt at the fabulous blue air. Layers of browns and blacks. Forest green moss playing peek-a-boo from underneath. She had a sudden fierce pang of regret. A longing to be sitting at their old kitchen table in the city, reading the paper and drinking a latte, hearing traffic, maybe a siren.

Sitting on the cool plastic seat, she scratched out a diamond shape on the wall with her thumbnail. She didn't think winter would be this hard. She took the toilet paper off the nail and pulled off three squares. It was almost four full months they'd been out here, their six-year anniversary together.

Just last week, after Mark had come home from work and washed himself with hot water from the black pot, he approached Colleen from behind while she was shredding carrots for a salad. The scent of his naked arms was tinny from the cast iron, the smell of a rail yard. He slid her pink cargo pants past her hips and ran his tongue along the deep curve of her lower back. He took the shredder from her hand and turned her body into his. She was wearing an old shapeless tank top that would have easily torn had he chosen that, but instead he pulled both sides of the top together, clutching the fabric in a fist at her sternum, exposing her on both sides. He bent down and rubbed his eyelids over her left breast and found her nipple with his teeth. With his free hand he used the length of his thumb to slowly trace the sensitive crease underneath.

Later, when they had crawled up to the loft, Mark slept with one hand balled up under his chin, his other hand curled around his own fist. His breath was low and even, rising up from his belly. He was healthier here. Maybe this was the right thing. If she were to paint this, she would start the piece with the shade of blue between dusk and darkness, a heavy colour on the verge of change, and let the image burst out in fiery yellows and oranges, vivid strokes of resilience and battle.

In the time it took her to use the toilet, the sky had clouded over. Even the weather was suffocating her. She undid the scarf from her neck, folded it diagonally, and tied it around her head. Where were Mark and Gary? She went back inside and took two apricots from the bowl on the table.

"We need a break, you and me," she told the duck.

She placed the fruit in the side pocket of her cargo pants, took their binoculars off the back of the door, and looped the leather strap over her shoulder. A brisk walk in the woods would clear her head.

Steph had ended up on the cash-only, tax-free payroll of an undisclosed logging company through a web of unorthodox connections. Tit for tat was their philosophy. If there was no paper trail on either side, everyone would get along just fine.

To them, she was "Big Becky flying her Red Robin Delivery Bird." Sometimes, after she had unloaded the delivery, she would stick around and play cards. She'd take their money, tell a few nasty jokes, and suck back the whisky they offered before she headed out to the plane.

"That's it for me, fellas, you've been great," she'd say. "See you in church."

Away from Daisy, there were days she ate nothing but bacon. Two pounds of it throughout the day, washing it down with four or five Kokanees. Alone at night, she poked the fire, read, slept, and pleasured herself. She would go outside and rub against the rough bark of a tall spruce. She would hook a finger inside and wiggle it around until she came. Usually she ended up doing a few sets of pushups to expel the excess energy. After, she would shake her head to loosen her neck and shoulders.

The land was alive down there. Trees lined up like arteries, breaking off into veins and capillaries. Snow-capped mountain peaks were nipples, pinched white. Hills were freckled with shadows and imperfections, and rivers flowed like untamed hair. Over the radio, she got a clearance of 200 feet and angled the steering wheel of the Red Robin southbound, toward Gibson's Landing.

Brooke had wanted to cut her hair like Steph's crewcut and kept insisting until Daisy finally took her to a salon. She was not going to allow Steph to hack away at their daughter's hair with the blade she used to cut her own. Daisy also vetoed a dye job. Brooke had read the entire Lemony Snicket collection, and even though she was mature for her age, a platinum-blonde six-year-old was too much for Daisy to take.

"She's hardly a baby," Steph said.

"She's hardly an adult," Daisy said.

Daisy had been right, of course. She was right about how much calcium they were all getting. She was right about limiting the amount of screen time Brooke got. She was right about using coasters on the new pine coffee table.

Looking down at the river, it was not always clear which direction things flowed, large to small or the other way around. And it was while Steph was pondering this thought, the engine starting making noise. Rough, loud, breaking sounds that were far from normal. The entire aircraft started to vibrate, shaking her in her seat.

There had been warnings about cougars. She was supposed to make loud noises on the trails to deter the wild cats, so Colleen belted out random song lyrics, anything she remembered.

"I am just a poor boy, though my story's seldom told!"

She was thirty-two, living in a wooden box with her unpredictable lover.

"This land is your land, this land is my land!"

She placed her glasses on a rock and adjusted the focus of the binocular lenses.

"Bismillah! No! We will not let you go. Let him go!"

She had given up drinking with Mark, and the absence of alcohol in her system made Colleen feel like she was filled with pockets of air. There were times she had trouble catching her breath. Lately her restlessness was paired with the lightness of boredom and a residual city anxiety. Anticipating things that had vanished from her routine—social events, appointments, deadlines. She had tried meditating, but when she sat still for too long her mind filled with images of the city. She tried to bowl them up in soft gauze and let them float into the clouds, a technique she'd learned at a workshop back in Vancouver, but they never went away.

"Hello darkness, my old friend!" she sang.

Through the binoculars she spotted an eagle surveying the surroundings from the top of a tree like a drug lord. The look in the bird's eyes said, "Face it, I'm superior."

In their old neighbourhood, she would cycle slowly past the houses, looking in people's windows illuminated by kitchen lights. Dusk was the best time for this. Once she caught a glimpse of a man shouting behind the glass. He reached out and took an arm, presumably of a woman, held it up, pulled it into another room. This was something she could use. Her abstract way of making sense of things. A canvas, chunky with underlays of burgundy and rust, streaks of orange running through it all and gathering in a pool at one edge, falling off, out of control. It was bold pieces like that that got her noticed in the city's arts community. She had been featured in the *Vancouver Sun* last fall after her show at the Elliot Louis Gallery.

"Good morning, good morning!" she sang, "We've slept the whole night through! Good morning, good morning, to you and you and you and you." A new level of lunacy in her solitary confinement.

When Colleen and Mark had lunch at Gary and Lila's last month (they were never invited for dinner), Lila gave the kids anything they wanted, clattering around in the kitchen the whole time. She cut open a crinkly bag of Cheezies and dumped them on a plate. They were the same colour as her damn duck.

"They get these on special occasions," Lila said.

"What is today?" Mark asked.

"Saturday, right, Poopsie?" She ruffled Ethan's hair with her fingers.

"Seriously?" Mark said. "Why aren't they eating real food?"

Gary had made a pot of homemade chili with organic beef from the city and green peppers he had grown himself. He seasoned it with cumin and smoked paprika and it smelled like a little café on Commercial Drive in Vancouver where Colleen used to go to eat lunch and sketch.

"They can have that anytime," Lila said.

"Except while they're young and growing and they need it," Mark said.

"Wait until you have kids," Gary said, and went back to eating his chili.

That was why she loved Mark. Even with his faults—the fitfulness, his short attention span—there were no games. He was direct, resolute, passionate.

While Lila scooped heaping spoonfuls of microwaved SpaghettiO's into plastic bowls for the kids, Colleen stirred her own bowl of chili. When they were done, Lila unwrapped a chocolate jellyroll and plunked it on the table along with an aerosol can of whipped cream. Chelsea applauded. Ethan reached for the can, leaned his head back, and sprayed the foam straight into his mouth.

"Ethan!" Gary said. "Can. Down."

Lila giggled. "Oh, he just loves that stuff."

Colleen had excused herself to use the bathroom, taking advantage of the flush toilet. She washed her hands and pushed her face into the hand towel, stretched her mouth into a silent scream.

Now, through the binoculars, beyond the trees, the eagle was still surveying its realm. Sleek and raw, the bird didn't have to try and be anything it wasn't. She should get rid of that duck. Replace it with an eagle. Past the bird, Colleen spotted a small red and white plane below the clouds. It looked like it was flying too close to the trees.

The eagle raised its head. A sharp turn to the left. White feathers damp from the mist stood out on the back of its neck. Colleen lowered the binoculars and picked up her glasses just in time to see a flash of red and white drop from the sky.

The vibrations were quickly getting worse, but Steph's breathing remained even. She was being tested. Not a single stressed muscle in her body. The path that had led her here was the right one. Whatever mechanical breakdown was happening, Red Robin (C-ROIB) knew the way; the plane was her best friend. It gave her more pleasure than any human ever had. Flying like this now, even within the turmoil, she couldn't imagine calling any other place home.

The vibrations became violent, and Steph's body hit the side of the aircraft. She started emergency procedures by lowering the airspeed to sixty knots. The action was automatic, beyond thinking. She reached over and pulled the black carburetor heat lever all the way out to the ON position. Establish a landing area. Yeah, right. A good pilot would have a field in mind, at least a road. *Damn it.* Her vision was skewed from the chaos in the cockpit, and the rows of evergreens below, which moments ago seemed like pillars of strength and domination, were now indestructible statues blocking her way. It had been only seconds since the vibrations started, but it felt like an eternity. She gripped the steering column to steady herself.

"Come on, Robin," she said. "We can do this."

Bang!

The shaking stopped. It was instantly silent. Wind rushing by her window was the only sound she could hear. In the strange and sudden quiet, she angled the aircraft left, performed a teardrop, and forced the plane to lose altitude.

She bit down hard on her tongue. Tangy and pungent, the taste of iron mixed with her saliva. The smell of avgas assaulted her. Nauseated, she took a deep breath and held the steering column as if she were on a Sunday afternoon drive. Still in the left tilt, she angled the right rudder for drag. Tried for thirty degrees but no luck. She was at twenty, if that. Steph pulled the mixture lever all the way out for fuel cut-off. No time left to get her nose down any further without increasing airspeed. Here it came.

Master switch, OFF.

Steph let go of the column with her right hand to grab the grey sweatshirt from under her seat. Anything to protect her face upon impact. Treetops tickled the bottom of the aircraft. *Fucking hell.* A drumming ticker tape keeping time beneath her. Both hands back on track, she blinked long and hard, clenched her face, her lips, her eyes. She reached over and cracked the door open. Steph lifted the nose, angled toward what was once a blue and cloudless sky, and applied all the air breaking power she could.

"Stall, baby, stall for me now," she said.

She was a ribbon, floating, a feather, a piece of string, falling earthbound.

A sick metallic thud echoed by a mammoth crunch brought her to stillness. Beyond black it was surprisingly light. A perfectly fluid spring day, the yellow guts of daffodils, lilacs, fragrant and sweet, drifting in and out.

Colleen didn't even have a cell phone with her. Or water. Would she have to go back and ask Lila for help? Did she even remember how to do CPR?

She moved like a hunchback, barely getting through the trees, protecting her face with her arms from rogue limbs sticking out at awkward aggressive angles. Whoever was in that plane could very well be dead by the time she got there. She established a rhythm. Recited the old sing-song chant from army movies, "I don't know but I've been told." She huffed the words out loud and picked up her pace. Everything started to get lighter, faster, brighter. She was practically running. Then she lost her footing on a small incline, and her left ankle gave out. A rush of adrenaline swept through her body. She leaned forward to regain her balance and a pine branch scraped along her cheek, tearing deeply into her skin.

"Fuck a duck," she said.

She pulled the scarf off her head and dabbed it on the cut, then shoved it in the pocket of her pants. She regained her momentum and navigated the terrain like an obstacle course, sweeping through the branches with breaststrokes.

When it was all over, Steph was penetrated by stillness. A place where the only movement was in the mind. She waited. Nature itself seemed to pause. The trees stood at attention with a respectful salute. A chipmunk froze in place. Thick and weighted, drops started to fall from the clouds. A soft, wet coolness swept over Steph, and she closed her eyes, listened to the rain.

One rainy October day, Brooke had one of her little friends over to the house. The friend was named after a place—Brazil? France? She had read a book to the girls: Dr. Seuss's *One Fish Two Fish Red Fish Blue Fish*. Steph was lying on her stomach on the area rug, and Brooke was perched on her backside. Rain drummed on the living room window. The other little girl sat cross-legged next to them. Her knee touched Steph's shoulder. The girls knew the story by heart; they'd heard it a hundred times. On page seventeen, France counted her fingers while Steph read. She turned the page, and Brooke reached over, put her hand on the seven hump Wump; she wanted to look at the image just a little longer. As she continued to read, Steph felt the little girl lightly touch the top of her hair. They mouthed the last words of the book along with Steph.

Steph knew what it should feel like to move her toes. Foot against boot. But there was nothing. Everything was liquefying, freezing. She dreamed she was floating in a pool of warm mineral water and sank into the healing elements, her skin smooth and slippery as she ran a hand up her arm, massaged her left shoulder. Magnesium and bromine. The steam smelled faintly of the earth, like a lawn after the rain. She shifted her jaw and tried to swallow.

Sometimes the loggers would offer her soup and stale bread. Horrid brown liquid with cardboard-coloured peas floating around the bowl and clumsy chunks of venison on the bottom. They spiced it with too much salt and pepper. What she wouldn't give for a sip of that awful soup right now. A cup of hot chocolate. A stick of Big Red. Steph ran her tongue across the back of her top teeth. The sickly metal flavour was everywhere. Every follicle was at attention. Her nipples were like wooden pegs under her shirt. The sky was light grey and it started to drizzle. She could still blink, and behind her eyelids was an icy darkness. She breathed out heavy through her nose, like a dragon. Some dragon. Her breathing got quicker, spurts from her nose, mucus sprayed out in shots, short and panicked. There was some blood. The condensation in the cockpit turned the windshield into a vapour-covered sheath. A chill on the back of her neck crept to the top of her skull like hands cradling her head in their icy clutches. A fish, red or blue, swimming slower and deeper and colder, until it was still as a rock.

It was not clear to Colleen what had led her down this path that wasn't even a path at all. The closer she got, the thicker the pines. She continued over the uneven ground where roots like massive tire treads grew out of nowhere and she climbed over them. Pushed through like a boxer. She was fighting for that person at the end of the line. She was fighting, she realized, for herself. Fighting to make a difference out here, to be of some use. As she approached the wreck, she took a deep breath. Tears slid into the wound on her face, and she felt the cut, hot and prickly, needling her flesh.

The pilot was pinned between the console and the seat, her shoulders slumped forward, compressed in the small cockpit. The woman had short blonde hair, an angular face. She looked younger than Colleen. Out here, crushed between a dashboard of levers and a navy leather seat, she looked like a child. The windshield was shattered but still intact and fogged up. It smelled like gasoline. Colleen pried the door open as far as she could. She reached in and put a hand on the woman's shoulder. Even if she were able to move, there was no way to get her out.

"I should go get help," Colleen said.

"It's empty," the woman said. "I was going home."

The woman's face had a pale grey sheen to it, not unlike the sky above them. There was blood at the corner of her mouth. When she opened her eyes briefly, they were shiny, like the reflection off plastic wrap pulled tight. They widened momentarily and she looked bug-eyed and exaggerated, like a fish in a pet store aquarium trying to escape from its own tank.

There was a dark red stain the size of a brick on the woman's side, just under her ribs. Colleen took off her vest, folded it, and worked it through the space between the woman's belly and the control panel that she was pinned against. She was very pretty. Their faces were close enough that Colleen could have leaned in and kissed her on the lips as she positioned the vest against her wound.

"Tell me a story," the woman said.

Colleen reached into her pocket for a tissue. The apricots.

"Do you want a piece of fruit?"

The woman squinted at her as if she didn't speak English.

"I want a story."

Colleen held the two apricots in her hand. Circled them around each other in her palm like her Chinese baoding balls.

"I went to Guatemala once. Spent a few days in a hostel on Lake Atitlan. One of those off-the-beaten-track places where people go, like Thailand, or here, I guess. There was a lot of pot and philosophy and anti-establishment music like Lou Reed."

The woman moaned; it was almost inaudible.

"There was this guy there from San Francisco. After his mother died, he cut off all his hair and told me how he took all the money she had left him out of the bank. It was like ten grand or something and he cut it up into little pieces and threw it out the window of his apartment. Like confetti. It made a huge mess and someone called the cops. When they showed up, he told them it was a ceremony from the Native side of his family that he was obligated to do, his mother's final wishes. How all things had to be returned to the earth. 'It's what she wanted,' he told the police."

The woman's face was slick with sweat. Colleen reached in and patted the woman's forehead with her scarf.

"He'd hitchhiked down to Mexico and ended up in Panajachel."

Rain danced on the roof of the plane. A crow cawed, the sound sliced through the air like a sword.

"It wasn't supposed to end like this," Colleen said.

"It's okay," the woman said.

"My boyfriend is a recovering heroin addict," Colleen said. "We're living illegally on his brother's property and trying to have a baby."

"I had a girl, once."

The woman had a dime-sized birthmark on her temple the colour of wet sand.

"I'm so sorry," Colleen said.

The woman's breathing had turned to wheezing. Colleen reached over and touched her spiky blonde hair. It was softer than it looked. Years later, Colleen would remember this exact moment. The cool rain, grey sky, and the woman's thin voice. "Israel," she said.

"What?"

"My daughter's friend's name was Israel," she said. "They called her Izzy for short."

The woman's shoulders were angled forward in a way that looked unnatural. Her muscles relaxed, more than a body should be allowed.

"What should I do?"

The rain was beating down on them now. Cleansing the wreck. Baptizing it. Colleen lifted her face and let the water hit her. Drops landed on her glasses, creating puzzle pieces that didn't fit anywhere. There was an unnatural smell. Gas. Death crawling in.

"You can't picture it until it's happening," the woman said.

"I'm here," Colleen said.

Colleen's tears mixed with the rain on her face. One day she would paint this. Dark greens and light greens, grey with slashes of red. Colleen wasn't heaving or sobbing, she was simply crying for this woman. Crying for the child that might have a chance inside her. Crying for Mark. Crying for the inevitability of their leaving this place and trying again somewhere else.

Colleen saw the mother first. She was as big as Gary's truck, plodding her way along the side of the mountain opposite them. The big brown bear stopped and swiped at her face with a huge wet paw.

"Oh, look," Colleen said.

Twenty feet behind the bear was a cub. Clumsily tripping forward, its head no bigger than a softball.

"Hmm?"

It took everything the woman had left to lift her head to an angle that would let her see the animal. Colleen helped. She held the woman's neck in such a way that she could see the cub trailing in the path of its mother. The crash must have startled them. They were on the move. Looking for food, or possibly a different way home.

Acknowledgments

I would like to express my profound thanks and appreciation to the fine folks at Arsenal Pulp Press, Brian Lam, Susan Safyan, Gerilee McBride, and Cynara Geissler, for their enthusiasm, patience, and editorial care that has gone into this book.

This collection would not exist without Sarah Selecky. Her unwavering support and encouragement is unparalleled. She has been there from the beginning: cheering, steering, inspiring, laughing, believing.

I am grateful for and indebted to the wonderfully wise and brilliant: Zsuzsi Gartner, Annabel Lyon, Denise Ryan, and Jessica Westhead for exceptional insight, advice, and influence.

Thank you Cinnamon Karma (Chris, Pam, Rami) and The Molly Blooms (Adam, Jasmine, Jason) for careful reading and constructive feedback. And cake.

Three cheers for Jeffrey Vanderby who has read these stories almost as many times as I have.

Friends, family, peers—near and far—you know who you are, and I will thank you in person when I see you.

My parents, Ted and Margaret Starchuck, led by example: curious and fun-loving people who insisted on looking up words in the dictionary. They instilled a love of reading early on, and I thank them for that, and everything else.

All my love and gratitude goes to my husband David for keeping me inspired, entertained, and grounded. And for reminding me to, within the noise and the clutter, take a break, and look up.

LANA PESCH is an alumnus of the Banff Wired Writing Studio and her short fiction has been published in *Little Bird Stories: Volumes I* and *II*. She was longlisted for the 2014 CBC Short Story Prize and won the Random House of Canada Creative Writing Award at the University of Toronto in 2012. *Moving Parts* is her first book. She lives in Toronto.